PRAI

MW00812044

"In time-hopping tales of lust, lunacy, and intrigue, *Ending in Ashes* burns bright with inspired story-telling. Rewinding from present day through a number of historical eras, Jones-Howe draws on the genre conventions of gothic romance and paranormal mystery to make a larger statement about the horrors of the patriarchy, though never at the expense of keeping us entertained. The stories sizzle, the writing dazzles. It's a winning combo of deadly secrets, carnal thrills, and sharp social commentary that is sure to set your senses ablaze."

NATHANIAL BLACKHELM, AUTHOR OF
LITTLE BLACK CRIMES

"Before you pick up *Ending in Ashes*, be aware that it isn't a collection of short stories; it's a study in heart-break, longing, and rage. Horror of the highest calibre, Rebecca Jones-Howe's writing will leave you breathless, broken, and begging for more."

CAITLIN MARCEAU, AUTHOR OF *THIS IS
WHERE WE TALK THINGS OUT*

"To call this powerful collection of stories gothic horror, well, that's the tip of the iceberg—the rest of the darkness, despair, and longing are hidden from view. If there is a line, Rebecca will cross it; if there is a sickness, she will expand it; if there is a looming fear, she will embrace it. Not for the faint of heart, we are mutually destroyed in these whispered secrets."

RICHARD THOMAS, AUTHOR OF
SPONTANEOUS HUMAN COMBUSTION,
DISINTEGRATION, AND *BREAKER*

"*Ending in Ashes* is a darkly beautiful collection of stories about broken people, ghosts, and the ghosts of broken people. A menacing, claustrophobic journey through timeless narratives of shattered and dysfunctional love. Jones-Howe expertly leads the reader into places they don't want to go but can't look away from. She will leave you devastated."

JESSICA LEONARD, AUTHOR OF
ANTIOCH AND *CONJURING THE WITCH*

ENDING IN ASHES

ENDING IN ASHES

A SHORT STORY COLLECTION

REBECCA JONES-HOWE

EDITED BY
CASSANDRA L. THOMPSON

ENDING IN ASHES: A SHORT STORY COLLECTION
BY REBECCA JONES-HOWE
PUBLISHED BY QUILL & CROW PUBLISHING HOUSE
EDITED BY CASSANDRA L. THOMPSON

Cover Design by Dennis Ramirez & Fay Lane

Interior by Cassandra L. Thompson

Printed in the United States of America

ISBN (ebook): 978-1-958228-35-7

ISBN (paperback): 978-1-958228-36-4

Cataloging-in-Publication Date is on file with the Library of Congress

Publisher's Website: www.quillandcrowpublishinghouse.com

To my dear cousin Dean Mark. You told the best dirty jokes and I will miss you always.

CONTENTS

INTRODUCTION

REBECCA JONES-HOWE

I used to swear I'd never write anything set in the past. I got my start in transgressive fiction. My goal was simply to write dark stories with a feminist edge. For a while, I did that well. I published my first collection, *Vile Men*, in 2015. For a debut, I think it went well. It's hard to generate buzz around a short story collection, but *The Globe and Mail* called it a "nuanced collection taking a smart twist on dark genres" and I was pleased.

Then I went and I had a kid.

Postpartum depression broke me for a bit, and so I spent a couple of years hiding out, yellow wallpaper-style, wrestling out all my angst into a novel about the isolating world of millennial motherhood. Convinced that it was the next *Gone Girl*, I queried it for a year. Many of the agents who rejected it did so with insightful comments. They considered the book "gothic", which was a genre I'd never really considered my work fall into. However, looking back at all the media I consumed growing up (Disney's *Beauty and the Beast*, and V.C. Andrews's *My Sweet Audrina*, and yes, so much Sylvia Plath), a lot of the subjects I wrote about just made sense.

Things like isolating environments. Questionable decision-making. Sexual tension. Gender politics. Internal angst. And yes, sinister men who double as love interests.

Covid hit, and I found myself trapped in my house with

my children day after day. My only reprieve was staying up until the wee hours of the morning, revising my novel to query a second batch of agents. The feedback I got was better, and then, finally, an agent called, suggesting a rewrite before they felt comfortable accepting. I eagerly spent the end of 2020 hastily revising the book. Once I sent it, I distracted myself by writing short fiction again.

Short fiction is my first and true love. This time, however, I broke tradition by writing stories set in the past, stories that were verbose and lyrical. These stories were a much-needed break from the modern world I often wrote about, as well as the modern world I was quite sick of living in.

But then, come April of 2022, the agent had a response. Rejection. I took it hard, alone in my house in the middle of a pandemic. Fortunately, my kids were there to hug me in that raw moment of emotion, but I still had more to process on my own.

Covid vaccines were rolling out, and I lined up to get my shot around a bunch of super excited people. I got my shot, then sat in a hard chair of the auditorium, waiting the required 15 minutes to see if the vaccine would give me any negative side effects. I pulled out my phone and read that rejection email over and over, expecting the worst, and then the worst never happened.

I walked out of the auditorium, now immune to the dangers of the world.

I'd never been more depressed in my life.

I suppose that's the worst part of getting rejected, expecting the world to swallow you whole, when, ultimately, you're just sitting there, everybody around you smiling, not understanding what was lost. Time. Energy. Passion. Dreams. It's probably the most isolating part of being a writer. You just have to sigh, absorb the loss, and figure out what to do next.

I wrote another story. Then another. Then another. It was easy. Cassandra and the fine folks over at Quill & Crow Publishing House kept asking for more stories. Writing them provided an escape. I got the serotonin boosts I so desperately needed. I wrote enough stories to put together a second collection of short fiction. And here it is, a selection of gothic tales that connect our current hellscape to hellscapes of the past. Stories about characters like myself, or perhaps characters like you, people stuck in moments in time, in situations they'd rather not be in, forced to make choices. Trapped. Making the best of it, or, in some cases, the worst.

One of these days, I'll fix my rejected novel. Or, maybe it'll remain trapped within the world of my hard drive, never to see the light of day. I do what I can to survive in my predicament, every night toiling to shed perspective. It's making the best in the worst of times, honestly.

In the meantime, I hope you enjoy the collection. I worked really hard on it.

FOREWORD

CASSANDRA L. THOMPSON

I'm sorry, Rebecca, but I hated "Woman of the White Cottage."

Let me explain. It was early 2021, and I had just embarked on my first anthology as the editor-in-chief of my newly established publishing house. The call was unusual, but one true to my nerdy self: I wanted some Gothic medical horror.

When Rebecca Jones-Howe appeared in my inbox, I gave her story a read like any other. I was immediately drawn in by her distinct prose and creative use of repetition/symbolism, and soon I found myself deeply invested in the character Mary. A few pages in, however, I couldn't continue. Deeply unsettled, I put my computer down and got up to get a glass of water.

Over the next few days, I sorted through submissions, trying to ignore the little RJH icon in my inbox. After I was confident I'd compiled a solid anthology, I knew I had to go back to the "Woman" situation.

Begrudgingly, I moved it to the rejection folder.

No, dammit, she's a brilliant writer!

I moved it to the acceptance folder.

You can't just accept it without knowing the ending!

And so, to end the war within my own brain, I swallowed my apprehension and finished "Woman of the White Cottage." After I read the last word, I took a long pause. Then the realization hit me. Rebecca had written true Gothic horror.

I've done numerous Gothic-themed submissions calls after that one, but plenty of writers miss the mark. Gothic horror isn't just about Victorian England and fancy words. It's really a collection of themes that, when put together, have created a genre that has survived the test of time. When considering Gothic fiction, one thinks of *Dracula* and *Wuthering Heights*, but not many realize stories like *The Shining* and even *Twilight* are also Gothic in their own right. It's an incredible genre to study, and its modern redefinition has proven fascinating.

In this spirit, with "Woman in the White Cottage" and other stories, Rebecca has created what we like to call 'Neo-Gothic' literature. Like her female predecessors, Rebecca takes the deep-rooted, universal fear in all women, and plays them to perfection against horrific, villainous men who have their own ambiguity. I hated "Woman in the White Cottage" because it shocked and appalled me. It made me squirm. I could see myself in Mary, and I can recall men just like Nathanial. What "Woman in the White Cottage" did to me was exactly what Gothic horror was born to do, so many years ago.

Rebecca continues to shock and amaze me in the most uncomfortable ways with every piece she has ever brought to me, and I'm honored to publish her short story collection. As an advocate for both women's history and the Gothic genre, I consider Rebecca one of my favorite writers. She takes elements both horrific and erotic, and twists them in a way that leaves you unceremoniously unsettled...but contemplative. She explores a fear that has plagued women since the dawn of time: being helpless at the hands of 'vile men.'

It is my hope that you will take something from this collection as I have, and enjoy the natural talent that is Rebecca Jones-Howe.

CHAPTER 1

THE RED HOUSE

ORIGINALLY PUBLISHED IN "HAUNTED: A CROW SHOWCASE"

Annie had sent out the wedding invitations before the pandemic. A month passed in quarantine. Then Chris got himself wasted and called Annie a *cunt* for the very last time. She called her mother for help, though her mother lived out of town and had little to offer.

"What if you stayed with your Uncle David?" she suggested.

Annie hadn't seen her uncle in a while. He still lived in his partially restored heritage house downtown, its dilapidated siding peeling in slivers of deep red. Its handmade stained-glass windows revealed only darkness lurking inside.

Uncle David helped Annie load what few possessions she carried from her old life into her new normal, which was the furnished bedroom located on the house's main floor.

Annie lifted her duffel bag onto the sagging bed.

"We never got to renovating this room," Uncle David said, running his finger down the pale blue walls, the paint slathered thick and uneven. "Eliza wanted it to be her glass studio."

Annie peered through the yellowed lace curtain at the overgrown rose bushes. "I'm just glad I had a place to stay," she said, "with family."

Distant family. Removed family. Annie's connection to her uncle had ultimately died with Aunt Eliza, who ran her car into a highway meridian two years before.

Just the mention of her was enough to break his focus. He nodded and stared at the floor, then lifted his thumb to his teeth and bit down on the nail. "Emily's here too, you know."

"Oh," Annie said. "Mom never told me."

"Nobody knows," he said. "I pulled her out of rehab."

Annie swallowed. "Is she any better?"

"Not really." He buried his thumb into his palm, making a fist. "Some days she's better. She got a job at the grocery store. It's only part-time, but it keeps her busy."

"I haven't seen her in, well—" *Since the funeral*, Annie thought, but she wasn't about to mention the change that Aunt Eliza's death had brought upon Emily. She'd adopted her mother's collection of vintage clothes and perfected her mother's ability to abuse a bottle.

"She spends most of her time up in her room," Uncle David said. "My room's upstairs too, but you really don't need to go up there." He nodded at the door to the right. "There's a full bathroom right here. It's renovated. You'll like the bath. It's a clawfoot. Eliza found it at an estate sale once."

"I'm really grateful," Annie said.

Uncle David smiled. "It'd be nice if it were under different circumstances."

"It's fine," she said, but the unease still settled between them. The silence lingered for too long, and Annie took it upon herself to step forward, opening her arms for an embrace. It was important, now more than ever, to maintain a positive focus. She was grateful for an opportunity to leave, grateful for him—for family.

He hugged her back, arms over her shoulders, holding her in place for just a moment before letting go.

In the morning, Annie found the wedding invitation still posted on Uncle David's fridge.

She lifted the magnet to pry it off, and the RSVP card slipped to the floor.

She tossed the invitation in the recycling bin before making herself an espresso. The groan of the machine vibrated through the main floor's open layout. Its original walls had been taken down, allowing Aunt Eliza's stained-glass windows to cast a spectrum of light across empty space.

Between the living room and the kitchen stood a pool table, which Uncle David probably purchased post-divorce. The kitchen stood finished with white farmhouse-style cabinets. Annie placed her computer on top of the onyx countertop and pulled up a stool.

I'm grateful to have a place where I can safely work from home.

Her keystrokes echoed in the open space. It wasn't a comforting echo, but Annie posted her daily affirmation of gratitude as a means of instilling the new normal. Making it comfortable.

Uncle David walked the floor above, back and forth, the floorboards creaking. On the phone, probably. Work, probably. He said he had a little office in his room, a desk and a chair where he could work his public cases from home. His steps creaked slow, calm, steady.

Plotting steps.

Annie hesitated, watching the ceiling. None of the second floor was renovated. Construction supplies still sat under faded tarps in the backyard, and the uneven blue paint remained on what little she could see of the landing at the top of the stairs.

The front door creaked open.

Emily stepped inside, her hair longer, messier, her lips darkened like the exterior walls of the house. She wore one of her mother's vintage fur stoles, which she draped carelessly over the coat rack before digging a bottle out of her satchel. "Hey."

Annie smiled. "It's been a while."

"It has." Emily smiled back, her expression wiser but worse for wear. She bit her thumb just like her father. "So, you left Chris."

Annie nodded.

"I always thought Chris was an asshole."

"It took a while to get up the courage." Annie forced herself to laugh. "The whole pandemic thing kind of helped."

Emily glanced up the stairs where the creaking persisted.

"Your dad said you got a job," Annie said.

"I needed the money. They're paying an extra two bucks an hour. Hazard pay. It's okay. It's just good to be out of there."

"It's almost like a small family reunion," Annie said.

"In a way, I guess." Emily clutched at the bottle of vodka. Aunt Eliza's favorite. "I'm going to head up."

"Okay," Annie said. "We'll talk soon, okay?"

Emily nodded, her footsteps heavy. She banged the bottle between the balusters as she made her way upstairs.

I'm grateful for a fresh start.

A fog hung over the streets. Gray pressed against windows, dulling Annie's view of the overgrown backyard. The espresso machine growled, brewing Annie's second drink of the morning. Sounds creaked above her, and Annie turned to the stairwell where Uncle David emerged carrying a banker's box. He smiled and placed it on the pool table before brushing the dust off his slacks.

"Just clearing out some of Emily's things before heading to work."

"You're not working from home?" Annie asked.

"Nobody else is at the office. It's quieter and all my client files are there." He went to the machine to fill his Thermos with coffee.

Annie leaned over the table, glancing inside the box, which held several stacks of old V.C. Andrews paperbacks. She flushed and smiled, remembering the family reunions of her teens, all that time spent consuming the incestuous prose on the beach. Emily used to read the passages aloud, her voice registering in the open space. Annie dug into the box and pulled out a copy of *Midnight Whispers*.

"You want them?" Uncle David asked.

Annie shook her head. "Emily brought home alcohol last night."

"She's been doing it a while," he said. "She thinks I don't know."

"And you're okay with it?"

"She's quiet in her room. She sorts through things, and she tells me what to throw away." He motioned at the box. "I try to talk to her. She never wants to. But she's home," he said again. "And she's discarding things. It's all a part of the grieving process."

Annie held her breath instead of persisting, because it was already evident that Emily wasn't so much grieving as she was under the influence. Eliza's influence. Eliza's spell.

"I offered to spend some time with her," Annie tried.

Uncle David carried the box to the front door, burying his feet in his loafers. "We'll spend some time together this week, Annie. We'll cook. We'll talk more, okay?"

"Sure," Annie said. She forced a smile as the door closed, Uncle's David's shadow turning black behind the stained glass like a withered rose.

I'm thankful for fresh starts.

Annie found herself checking Chris's profile not long after. He'd changed his photo from a portrait of he and Annie, to a selfie of him drinking a beer. Annie straightened in the barstool, trying to shift the ache that weighed over her shoulders.

Uncle David had gone to the office again, though it wasn't long before another black shadow emerged. Emily stumbled over the doorway, her satchel slipping halfway down her arm, clogs thudding against the hardwood.

"Careful, Emily!" A man followed her, his gait the same. He stumbled over her, laughing with relief when he looked inside the satchel to find the bottle inside wasn't broken.

"This is Tony," Emily said.

"We're not supposed to have outside people in the house," Annie said.

Emily shrugged. "Dad won't mind. He let *you* stay."

"I'm not going anywhere else, though."

Emily headed for the stairwell, staring Annie down as she pulled Tony along. "You really shouldn't have come here."

"Why?"

"You know why," Emily said.

Annie exhaled, her spine curving. "Your dad's been really helpful."

Tony pointed. "Who is she?"

"She's my cousin," Emily said. "She just left her piece of shit abusive fiancé."

"For your *dad*?" Tony asked.

Emily grabbed his elbow and pulled him the rest of the way up the stairs.

Annie willed herself off the barstool. She tiptoed across the floor and peered upstairs at the thick coats of blue paint. The steps creaked beneath her hesitant ascent.

A red glare flashed along the wall.

"What are you doing, Annie?" Uncle David asked, easing the front door closed with his foot.

"Emily brought somebody home."

He set down the groceries and slipped out of his coat. "I wouldn't worry about it."

"Are you okay with strangers coming in here?"

He hung the coat over Eliza's vintage furs. "They went

straight upstairs, didn't they? They always do. Come and help me with the groceries."

Annie glanced up at the darkness.

"I promise you're safe down here, Annie."

She looked down at her uncle, trying to find comfort in his expression as she descended.

Annie's phone rang in the middle of the night.

"Please come home," Chris pleaded, voice sloppy. "I hate sleeping without you."

"I can't," Annie said. "I'm done, Chris."

"No, you're not."

She hung up, but the phone rang a second time. Then a third. She blocked his number, replacing his desperation with the footsteps above. She imagined Uncle David awake, walking back and forth across the room. She tried to imagine the reliable pace as a pattern, something to focus on. It only kept her heart racing, her limbs rigid, ready for anything.

She opened her computer, its bright screen casting glare against the window and all the threats outside.

I'm grateful for a sense of calm, she wrote, hesitating before pressing Post.

Uncle David showed Annie how to make broccoli beef stir fry. They ate over the kitchen counter, a lit candle between them to add some warmth to the rainy day.

"If there's anything you need, just let me know. And I'm not just talking about groceries," Uncle David said, stabbing at a slice of beef with his fork. "If it comes to you needing an attorney, I can refer you to one at the office—"

"It's not that bad," Annie said. She poked at the broccoli, her shoulders still tight from the night before. "Chris called, but he was drunk."

"What did he say?"

She shrugged. "Guys who get dumped always say the same thing."

Uncle David placed his fork on the plate, trading his next bite for the hangnail on his thumb. He chewed until Tony's car pulled up, its throbbing bass stereo shaking the delicate stained-glass. The front door creaked open, and Emily swayed inside, pulling off her wide-brimmed hat before closing the door.

A gust of wind slipped through the house, whipping at the candle between Annie and Uncle David. The flame flickered.

Emily narrowed her gaze at the unease. "Don't fuck my dad, Annie," she said.

Uncle David hammered his fist over the black counter. His fork slipped off the plate.

Emily heaved a laugh, then headed up the stairs.

"I'm sorry," he muttered. "She's not the same. I know she's not."

Annie's throat tightened. Her lungs ached.

Uncle David picked his fork back up.

The flame calmed as they ate in silence.

I'm grateful for a routine without guilt.

Working from home had no rules, so Annie closed her computer and poured a glass of red wine in the middle of the day. She ran a bath and lay in the embrace of the claw-foot tub, imagining Aunt Eliza in her place as the rain pattered the window beside her.

Annie placed the wine glass on the wicker chair next to the tub. She remembered buying it at an antique shop with her mother, once a birthday gift for Aunt Eliza. She reached out and scratched at a bead of red on the edge of the seat.

You're not safe here.

Her phone chimed. Her mother sent a screenshot of Chris's latest status update. He'd posted one of their engagement photos, the one where he held Annie in a soft embrace, her left hand draped over his shoulder, showing off the glare of the ring. Posed and fake and cheesy. It looked as though she was hanging off him for dear life.

This woman is the best thing that ever happened to me. She is my life, my EVERYTHING. I'd be NOTHING without her. I NEED her.

Annie drank a mouthful of the wine, imagining the red settling in the crevices of her teeth. She leaned back, letting her face slip beneath the warmth of the water.

He doesn't love you.

She appreciated the internal voice, the lack of guilt.

Then she rose to breathe. Water dripped off her nose and chin, trickled off the coiled ends of her hair. She reached for her phone again, noticing the shadow lingering beneath the bathroom door.

"Uncle David?" The floor creaked, and Annie took another swig of wine. "Emily?"

The shadow moved closer, listening as the water dripped. There were no creaks from upstairs, not like normal.

Annie climbed out of the tub and reached for her robe. Water trickled over the tiled floor, sounding frantic like her breaths. She tied the sash around her waist. "Emily, please don't mess with me."

The door rattled like a hand was pressed against it, fingers padding over the wood.

All that lingered on the other side was a feeling, a foreboding cold that kept Annie locked in the room. She turned to the window, more cut-glass roses, red petals, and brown thorns.

Another creak. The shadow beneath the door grew. The water chilled, pocking her flesh with goosebumps. Annie dragged the wicker chair to the window and climbed up. She slid the pane and wrestled herself through the opening.

Barefoot on the veranda, she pulled her robe tight around

her frame. Rain pounded around the house. She coiled her hair over her shoulder and twisted the water out, shivering in panic before peeking back in through the window where the shadow still stood.

The doorknob turned. The lock rattled.

Annie rounded the house to the front porch and squinted through the foggy glass. The window darkened, its rose turning black from the inside.

A hand touched her shoulder.

She cried out, shaking.

"Annie, what are you doing out there?" Uncle David asked. He gawked at her, then unlocked the door. "Come inside before you freeze."

She shook her head, glancing at the rainy street before slumping back against the house's siding. Shivers wracked her chest. Her sobs fogged in the cold.

Uncle David touched her shoulder again. "Come in, Annie. It's okay."

"Is it haunted?" she asked.

"What?"

"The house. There was something, *someone* at the bathroom door."

Uncle David glanced down the darkened hall.

"I swear I felt it," Annie said, but Uncle David only leaned in closer, his expression changing. She knew that he could smell the wine on her breath.

"It's not haunted," he said. "I've never felt anything but comfort here. Okay?"

Annie nodded, still uncertain.

"You're just scared," he said. "I don't blame you. Not at all."

She followed him back into the house. He closed the door. Locked it. He turned the light on, and her gaze went right for the top of the stairwell, where she was sure the shadows moved.

Movement woke Annie in the night. Creaks. Cries.

She ventured into the hallway, the rough cracks between the floorboards threatening to splinter the soles of her feet.

Emily appeared in the stairwell, dressed in a floor-length peignoir set. Steps hindered by alcohol, she wavered through the living room and caught her foot on the edge of the rug.

Fabric tore, echoing in the open space.

"Oh fuck," she moaned. She drew a breath and gathered the gown before stumbling into the kitchen for the last of the wine.

"Hey," Annie whispered.

Emily yelped, the bottle shifting in her grasp. She clutched it tight, her voice breaking as she lifted the long skirt to show Annie the tear in the lace. "I ripped Mom's nightgown."

"I know you miss her," Annie tried.

"She should have left him earlier," Emily whimpered. "Dad kept saying he'd change, but that's always bullshit, right? Men never mean it what they say."

"Sometimes they do."

Emily took a long swig and wiped her lips with the back of her hand. "I know you're smart, but you can't stay here. You shouldn't be spending time with him."

Annie lingered, gripping the counter's cold surface for support.

"He does shitty things when he's sad," Emily said. She took another swig and lost her balance, her elbow knocking against the counter. The bottle bashed against her lip. She moaned and wiped away blood.

Annie reached out, but Emily waved her off, gathering the skirt of the gown as she made her way back down the hallway toward her room.

A door creaked open at the top of the stairs.

Light cut across the shadows, and Annie knelt on the steps, watching as Uncle David's figure appeared.

"Emily, what are you doing?"

Her voice cracked. "You hurt Mom. I just want Mom back."

Uncle David sighed with his approach.

Emily lashed out with the bottle, the wine sloshing.

"Emily, calm down," he said. "Your lip's bleeding."

She struck again, but he twisted the bottle from her grasp. The glass crashed against the wall and shattered on the floor. Red over blue.

"Let me go!" Emily cried. She sobbed harder, but Uncle David held firm, dragging her back down the hall toward her room.

"You're drunk again," he said. "You're a mess."

Emily's cries faded as he closed the door. He made his way back down the hall, leaving the spilt wine and glass shards. Annie ventured up the next step to see around the corner of the landing, but her foot slipped behind her.

"Stay in your room, Emily!" Uncle David said.

Annie fell back, steps creaking. She darted across the open floor and hid beneath the pool table just as his figure leaned over the stairwell banister.

"Annie?" His voice had softened. "Annie, is that you?"

She covered her mouth and held her breath, watching as Uncle David eased, his shoulders dropping. He bit his thumbnail before turning back upstairs.

I'm grateful for quiet time.

Annie's mother liked the status update, but fewer people responded to her practice of positivity now, nearly two weeks after the separation went public.

The door opened, and Emily walked in. She stood straight, sober but with a new paper bag. She wore a black crochet cardigan over her grocery store uniform, the pale blue shirt poking through the loose stitches. It brightened her face, highlighting the flushed pink of her cheeks. She walked into the kitchen and set the new bottle on the counter. "You want to share some vodka?"

"I'm still working right now," Annie said.

"No, you're not," Emily said, glancing at the laptop. She bounced on her toes, her steps unburdened and her face brimming. She plucked a glass out of the cupboard and smiled.

Annie lowered her screen. "Just one, okay?"

Emily poured the vodka over ice, which clinked against the crystal as they raised their glasses. "To cousins and memories and female bonds," Emily said.

The vodka warmed their cheeks like campfire.

"Remember when your mom got us drunk that first time?" Annie asked.

"That wasn't my first time." Emily smiled, lips already wrestled loose.

Annie forced herself to swallow. "I'm sorry about your robe last night."

"What?"

"You ripped your robe when you came downstairs."

"Oh, yeah. I noticed that this morning. All I remember is Dad dragging me back into my room, honestly." She didn't look up again, just swished the vodka in the glass while holding her smile.

"Look," Annie said, "I'm not doing anything with him, if that's really what you thought."

"He's not even a blood relative," Emily said, shrugging. "You could fuck him if you wanted. Pretend it's like V.C. Andrews." She finished her drink and poured a second. She chugged the alcohol and laughed.

"What happened to you?" Annie asked.

"The same thing that happened to her." She picked at the flap of torn skin beside her thumbnail but lifted her glass instead of biting it.

"Why'd you even come back here?"

"I wanted to be closer to her," Emily said. "She has her own room upstairs. I borrow her clothes."

Annie stared at the black cardigan, Emily's hangnail catching in the yarn. "Do you ever feel like she's here?"

Emily shifted. "Dad put her ashes in an urn she would have hated."

"What do you mean?"

"It's this bullshit modernist wooden cube thing," Emily said. "I want to get her a proper one. I want to get her out of here and put her in the ocean like she wanted."

Annie finally sipped at her diluted vodka. The glass left a ring on the black counter and she wiped it away with her sleeve.

"You should come with me," Emily said.

"Where?" Annie asked.

She shrugged. "Tony's trying to help me find a place. Doesn't matter what it looks like, really. It'll still be better than here."

"But the pandemic—"

"It didn't stop you from moving away from Chris, did it?"

Annie hesitated.

"You can't stay here," Emily warned.

Annie stared at the ceiling of her room, the creaking above replaced with the sound of somebody pounding on the front door. Hard. Angry.

"Annie, I know you're there!" Chris yelled. "Your car's on the street!"

She climbed out of bed and lingered in the hallway—her reflection frozen in the door.

Chris pounded again. Yelled again.

Annie winced but forced herself forward. She turned the deadbolt, opened the door just wide enough to stare him down.

Chris stumbled over the doormat, breaths labored.

"I'm not coming back," she told him.

"You have to give me another chance!" He slapped his hand against the glass.

"Nobody's going to come to the wedding," she said, pushing her weight over the door. "This whole pandemic is a sign more than anything—"

He shoved her back, elbowing his way over the threshold, knocking the coat rack aside. Weighted by fur coats, it fell muted to the hardwood floor. Chris grunted and reached for Annie.

"Get out!" she screamed. "This isn't your house!"

"It's not yours, either! You have your own home and your own life and your own fucking bed where you should be sleeping!" The anger shifted through his jawline. His neck tensed but he steeled himself, staring her down. "This whole thing is stupid. I apologized for calling you a cunt. I always fucking apologize when I do something wrong!"

"I don't care!"

Chris lunged and Annie turned. She darted for the stairwell, but he swiped at her sleeve and yanked her around.

He sneered. "You still love me. I know you still care. Nobody just up and leaves like that."

"Of course, they do! I fucking did!"

He shook her and screamed, whiskey breath burning tears in her eyes. He made a fist, but the upstairs light flicked on to reveal Uncle David's shadow.

Chris staggered back, shielding his eyes from the glare.

"Go to your room, Annie," Uncle David said.

"It's fine," she gasped. "I'm okay."

Chris backed onto the doormat, but Uncle David rushed down the steps, grabbing the collar of his jacket before he could run. Chris thrashed. He threw a punch, but Uncle David seized his elbow.

Annie gasped, backing into the dark of the hall, hearing a whisper, a warning.

Leave now.

"I'll talk to him, Annie," Uncle David said. "I'll talk him down."

"Fucking prick!" Chris yelled.

"Just go to your room," Uncle David said, leaning his weight over Chris's drunken form. "Lock your door. It's going to be okay. I promise."

Annie backed herself into the shadows, her skin going numb as she obeyed.

I'm grateful for the protection of family.

Annie spent her next workday stalking Chris's recent activity. He'd changed his profile photo again. Just one of him in front of his truck. Gone were the desperate updates and any trace of Annie. At night, she sat on her bed and scrolled through the tamed Chris over a bottle of wine. He posted more than usual. Normal things. Everyday things. Her phone screen cast shadows in her bedroom. It wasn't until she heard the knock at the door that she glanced over.

The shadow lingered beneath. It breathed. It knocked again.

"Please stop," she begged.

The knob shifted.

No.

Annie sat up in bed, watching the shadow move. Another gentle knock, but Annie kept her lips tight, and her breath held.

A noise sounded. An echo in the blue walls.

He's coming.

Leave now.

Annie pressed her hand over her mouth, listening as the footsteps moved above her. She wanted to call for Uncle David. Her lungs ached. Her fingers shook. The door shook with her, its heavy walnut rattling against the metal hinges, hammering a sound of urgency.

Uncle David showed Annie how to make vodka sauce from scratch: crushed tomatoes in the food processor, blended to a bright red, then drizzled over chicken and fusilli.

Annie typed: **I'm grateful for second chances** before pulling two china plates from the cupboard. She served dinner with Aunt Eliza's antique silverware, its luster lost to years of neglect.

Uncle David pulled out a bottle of merlot and poured two glasses. "This was the first meal I made for Eliza."

Annie nodded, picking up her fork as Uncle David settled into his chair. He waited for Annie to cut into her chicken, to properly get a taste. She chewed but all she could do was nod and smile, thinking of all the V.C. Andrews men Emily laughed about, always stumbling and scary and obsessed with sheer nightgowns.

"She made me take cooking lessons," he said. "She made me a better man."

"It's good," Annie lied, because she tasted nothing.

The candle flickered and Uncle David stared at the flame. He shifted his thumb over his fork before shifting his jaw. "I did hit her," he confessed.

Annie reached for her wine.

His voice was low. Controlled. "It happened more than once. I know being drunk isn't an excuse. I know I was wrong. I treated her wrong." He raised his gaze but lowered it again, prodding the chicken a little before picking up his knife and cutting in. "I don't expect you to feel any different about me, Annie. I just thought it fair that you hear it from me. I know how Emily talks."

"She never said anything about what you did."

He chewed slowly, deliberately. "I wish I could fix it. I wish that being a changed person was enough."

The wine weighed down Annie's throat, thick and dark like blood.

"Is it all just words between you and Chris?" he asked. "He never hurt you, did he?"

The wine twisted in her stomach. "Emotional abuse is

still abuse, Uncle David." She pushed her plate to the side and tried to swallow.

He's coming.

He nodded, slicing through the chicken, the knife scraping over the plate.

Annie reached for the bottle and poured herself another glass.

The wedding invitation waited on the fridge in the morning, clipped back into place.

The joining in marriage of Christopher Daniel Weston and Anastasia Marion Clark.

Annie glanced at the emptied recycling bin, fighting the urge to lift the magnet and toss the expensive cardstock back into its blue depths.

Tony's car stereo blasted. A door slammed upstairs, and Emily hurried down with a suitcase and a large wicker beach bag. She grabbed what garments she could from the coat rack and shoved them inside as Uncle David's footsteps followed.

"I'm going to the ocean," she said, glaring at Annie. "You should come."

The music outside blared, shaking the stained-glass like church bells.

Annie glanced from Emily's determined glare to Uncle David's furrowed brows. "We're supposed to be in quarantine—"

"What exactly is he to you?" Emily asked, pointing at Uncle David. "Do you really think you're safe here? Do you really think he's got your best interests in mind?"

Uncle David stood at the top of the steps, gripping the banister. "Emily, please."

"Staying here is just prolonging the inevitable," she said.

The rattling continued, vibrating against the back of Annie's throat. Emily gripped the doorknob.

"Annie's not going with you, Em," Uncle David said. "Go ahead and leave if that's what you need to do."

The door slammed. The car revved. The music faded.

Uncle David descended the steps and turned the lock on the door, keeping Annie inside. Safe. He walked past her, brushing a hand over her shoulder on his way to the espresso machine. "You alright?"

Annie turned. "You said something about recommending an attorney before?"

Uncle David swallowed before nodding. "Of course."

Uncle David cooked spaghetti sauce for dinner, the fresh basil scent filling the house.

I'm grateful for comfort food, Annie typed, but a text message appeared from Chris.

> I'm NOTHING without you.
>
> Don't let one drunken word ruin what we have.
>
> Please!

Annie lit the candle on the kitchen counter. The flame breathed life, throwing light against the shadow lingering in the hallway, a ghostly hand reaching out.

Another text chimed.

> Stop being a fucking CUNT and answer me!

She held her breath, not wanting to look up, not wanting to see. She stared at the words until her eyes burned and her lungs ached.

"What's wrong?" Uncle David came around the counter, prying the phone from her hand. "I'm sorry, Annie." He tucked it into his shirt pocket and pulled her into his embrace. "I'm sorry. I'm so sorry. He's clearly not thinking straight."

She cried on his shoulder until the food was ready, served with wine. Annie ate until her appetite faded. She replaced her fork with the glass, her fear with anger. She slumped over the table and Uncle David tried to help her out of her chair.

"You're miserable," he said. "You need some time."

Leave now.

"Please don't touch me," she said, grabbing her phone from his chest pocket. She took it back to the bedroom, where the glow of Chris's words kept the shaking door at bay.

Annie woke to an empty house, her skull throbbing and the RSVP card still awaiting a signature when she went to turn the espresso machine on. She called for Emily, called for Uncle David. She glanced at the ceiling where the footsteps creaked back and forth.

Annie opened her computer, but the ache of her hangover prevented her from thinking of things to be grateful for. She moved across the floor and glanced up at the darkened stairwell.

The shadow moved out of view.

"What do you want?" she asked.

He's coming.

Aunt Eliza wasn't there. Aunt Eliza died in a car accident, drunk and alone.

Annie gripped the banister, willing herself to take one step at a time, to go where she was told not to.

The hallway narrowed. To the left stood Emily's vacated room, the bedsheets pried loose, and empty bottles scattered on the nightstand. Next was a cramped bathroom finished in the same sickly blue as the hallway. Uncle David's room stood open at the end of the hall, clean and tidy and minimal. A photo of him and Aunt Eliza sat on the dresser.

To the right was a closet, followed by the third bedroom, its door closed. Annie felt for the handle, expecting to touch cold, only to find warmth on the metal. She felt the presence waiting on the other side and swallowed.

She turned the knob. She pushed the door.

A slot of light pierced her eyes, and she squinted at the bars of clothing. Eliza's clothing, vintage and black and full of textures. Crochet and lace and fur. A trunk sat before her, flipped open and rifled through. Annie stepped into the room, the aroma of the vodka swelling in her nostrils.

He's coming.

The urn sat in the middle of the trunk, its bright wood finish so polished and so unlike her.

Eliza. Beloved Wife. Devoted Mother.

An omen. A presence. A foreboding return. Annie felt a hand on her back, willing her out of the room, wanting her gone, but she bent and picked up the urn. The lid flipped open. Dust slipped out but it wasn't enough. It wasn't all of her.

Annie brushed the ashes off, wiped her hands on her jeans, stumbling back on a pile of old coats Emily had left behind.

He's coming!

Leave now!

The voice growled in her temples and formed a migraine behind her eyes. She blinked out tears and stumbled from the room, but not before the door opened at the bottom of the stairs.

"Annie?" Uncle David called. "Annie, are you up there?"

Footsteps approached, more than one set.

Uncle David rounded the corner landing "I told you not to come up here," he said. Not angry. Not stern. Just concerned.

"I felt her," Annie said. "Emily took her ashes—"

"It's okay." He took her by the arm. "I made a mistake. We all make mistakes."

He's coming!

"Don't be angry with me," Uncle David said. "I'm just

trying to help." His grip tightened. Annie writhed, but he moved his hands to her elbows, holding her still when another shadow appeared on the landing.

Not that of Eliza, but of Chris.

He stood, cap in hand, his figure taking over the hallway, a smile forming, lips curving too high.

Annie shook her head. "No. No, please!" She wrestled out of Uncle David's hold, but she had nowhere to go.

"Give him a chance," Uncle David said, leaning over her shoulder as Chris approached. "Let him talk. Let him explain."

"No!" she cried.

Chris smiled wider, his teeth showing. A grin.

"You can go back home," Uncle David said. "You can make him better. Just listen to what he has to say, Annie. He just wants to make things right."

CHAPTER 2

HOSTAGES

ORIGINALLY PUBLISHED IN "EROS & THANATOS: AN ANTHOLOGY OF DEATH AND DESIRE"

Snow fell beyond the bistro window, thick heavy flakes drifting carelessly to the ground. Erin watched, hypnotized, unable to keep herself from clinging to the warmth of her coffee mug. Outside, cold tourists huddled together beneath patio heaters, hungry for the true experience of a mountain getaway. Erin preferred the indoors. She was grateful not to feel like the only person not acclimatized to their surroundings when a man entered the empty restaurant.

The bell announced him. He ordered a coffee and found a booth beside the window. He took no cream or sugar to mute the harshness of the brew. The bright snow contrasted his metal-rimmed glasses and his unkempt hair. Hunched over the table, he clasped at the hot ceramic of his mug, clinging like he needed the extra warmth. Clinging just like her.

It didn't take him long to notice Erin watching. His lips pursed. Then he did a double take and seized.

He remembered her.

Erin remembered that he'd smelt of gin, and that his throat had bobbed heavily when an armed robber entered the liquor store they happened to be in a year before. The man's voice was low and soft with a gentle rasp, and he'd told her to do whatever the robber asked. In the tension of the moment, he'd made Erin feel like her skin was vibrating. Back then, the man had a ring on his finger.

Erin had a ring too, but the robber left the store with it. She finally replaced her diamond engagement ring with cheap quartz from one of the many tourist shops in Whistler Village. The saleswoman told her quartz was good for clearing the mind of negativity, but all Erin could think of was her life coming unhinged the very moment she tossed her diamond into the robber's bag.

Across the room, the man took a drink, but the brew was still too hot. Coffee dribbled past his lip and down his chin. He wiped it with the back of his hand. Then he drew a heavy breath that strained his shirt over his chest.

Erin tensed, wanting to speak, wanting suddenly to move to the seat across from him, but the waitress approached his table with a slice of pie. The man jumped when she set it before him. She asked if he was okay, and he nodded too quickly, too vigorously.

"I'm fine. I'm alright."

Erin knew those words all too well—she had said them too many times, despite not meaning them.

The waitress left, and the man's panicked expression turned into something cold and grave and dead. Erin knew he was far from fine and far from alright. He fumbled with his wallet, swallowing hard as he retrieved the bills to pay for his meal. He pulled his jacket off the back of his chair and hurriedly shoved his arms into the insulated sleeves, zipping it quickly before leaving.

Erin watched him through the window as he paced down the bistro's front steps and through the village's chill. She made a fist and brought the quartz ring to her lips. Grating her teeth over the texture, she could still hear his voice in the ridges of the purple stone.

She chose not to follow him. There had been times since the incident when Erin felt like she was being followed. People treated her differently. Even her fiancé treated her differently, holding her hand extra tight whenever they shopped— which only worsened her anxiety, eventually making it hard to breathe in situations that should have been normal. Erin's fiancé often said he wasn't sure what to do. He felt helpless, which wasn't normal, which, in turn, made Erin feel as though she wasn't normal anymore. She'd been infected with something, a cold tension in her lungs.

She stopped allowing herself to be around people.

Being alone felt easier. She had moved out and got her own place, but the sky felt too big and all-encompassing. Her fiancé had begged her to do something that would help her overcome her trauma. Erin chose to travel to the snow-covered mountains of Whistler Village, where she hoped the clouded skies would feel like a proper ceiling.

The mountains were lined with ski lifts and gondolas taking people into the clouds. She watched the red glass-bottom cabins venture beyond the haze and wondered what waited on the other side. Everyone who plummeted back down did so with a smile, their cheeks flushed with excitement. Most of the tourists in the village carried skis or snowboards, leaving Erin to feel the blackness inside herself again.

She wasn't there for the same reason. She was different and wrong, and she was ill-prepared for the cold. So, she wandered the paved stroll between restaurants and shops, purchasing scarves and hats and little trinkets as souvenirs. In front of every shop entrance, there was a mass of blue de-icer. It was supposed to melt the snow but instead transformed it into a pile of blue sludge in the threshold, soaking into Erin's shoes, through her socks, and up the cuffs of her jeans.

She bought a pair of proper winter boots and returned to her hotel room, allowing her drenched denim to dry over the baseboard heater. She turned it up and then collapsed in the bed. The void of her phone ate up her afternoon. Erin searched for articles about the robbery, uncovering trauma she'd thought she'd buried. She remembered the robber's gun waving. She remembered her heart swelling in her throat, and that feeling of helplessness coming over her in the back corner of the store where the spirits were. She remembered the man with the glasses standing beside her in his gray suit.

He'd breathed heavily, already drunk and smelling of decay, despite carrying a briefcase, despite wearing a collared shirt and a tie. The robber made his way toward them and demanded their valuables. Erin's finger had swelled over the band of her engagement ring, making it impossible to remove. He fired a shot at the ceiling. Then another. Then the man with the glasses got between them. He held out a hand and tried to keep the robber calm.

"Nobody needs to die, alright?"

That soft rasp. That tingle in her throat. The ring had slipped out of Erin's shaking grasp, and the robber snatched it off the floor before firing one last shot directly into the man's chest. Erin remembered the smell of gin, the richness of blood, the chemical odor of bleach on the linoleum floor. She remembered the flashes of red and blue that burned her eyes as they loaded him into the ambulance.

She had scrolled the local news for days afterwards, hoping to read about whether he'd survived. Not knowing chilled her, made her grind her teeth, made her fingers shake. She'd started pretending she still had her ring, her fingers swelling as she simulated removing it over and over, hoping to do it faster, to bring the man back from the blackness in her head.

Erin woke to her phone ringing. It was her fiancé. She pushed the phone under her pillow and rolled groggily from beneath the covers. She went to the heater to see whether her jeans were dry but ended up pulling on a pair of sweatpants instead, along with her parka and toque. The ringing ceased, and she hurried from the room before he could call again.

She hated it when he worried. She could go out and enjoy herself, even if she was alone. She found herself at a nearby pub, where she sipped her gin and tonic in the corner, her eyes on the curling game on the television. Red rocks replaced the yellow rocks and then the yellow rocks replaced the red rocks, all while the players screamed back and forth mid-sweep. It only made her think of the robber yelling, of her chest caving in need to survive.

"Everyone get on the floor!"

The pub's floor was covered in melted snow, the muddy boot marks slick and slippery. A yellow sign was positioned over the worst of the slush, warning patrons of the hazard. Erin watched the tourists wander in and out, carelessly and drunkenly passing the silhouette of the man falling backward into a hopeless abyss. She finished her drink and brought the quartz ring to her teeth.

She closed her eyes and thought of diluted blood, could smell iron and gin as it twisted toward the nearest drain. On the screen, a yellow stone knocked a red stone out of play. The entire pub broke into cheer.

Erin couldn't make sense of the noise, so she left a twenty atop the table and walked back to the hotel, the crunch of snow like teeth grinding. She tried to unclench her fists, but all it did was expose her hands to the cold. She'd forgotten her gloves, so she rubbed her palms together in the elevator. She hurried down the hallway, digging through her pockets, unable to get a decent hold of the plastic keycard that would let her back into the privacy of her room.

The elevator chimed behind her. The doors opened and the man with the glasses walked out with a bag from the liquor store. He looked at her the same way he had in the bistro. His grasp tightened around the paper bag.

"Did you buy gin?" she asked, feigning normalcy.

"Yeah." He smiled for a moment, but looked down at her frostbitten fingers and swallowed, unable to hide his concern.

His suite overlooked the base of the mountain. The gondola sat motionless in the night, its cabins illuminated beneath the spotlights. Erin squinted, trying to see into the clouds overtaking the mountain, but its peak stretched too high and too far into the dark.

The man poured two drinks. Ice clinked against the glasses as he brought them to a small table in the center of the room. He sat across from her, swallowing again. He had a habit of swallowing, maybe even had before the robbery.

Erin studied his reluctance.

The vein in his neck twitched when he met her gaze. He shrugged out of his suit jacket, then turned to put it in the closet.

"I never thanked you," she said.

"You don't need to. The guy still got your ring in the end." The rasp in his voice picked at her throat, moved between her lungs and settled there. He took the seat across from her and emptied half the glass with a tilt of his head. "I see you've replaced it," he said, pointing to the quartz on her left hand.

"This is just tourist shit." She let go of her glass and slipped her hand beneath the table, out of his line of sight. "I'm just trying to do normal things and be a normal person. My fiancé worries."

The silence lingered. He glanced out the window and at the gondola. "My wife sent me to a therapist," he said before finishing his glass. "It didn't do much, just made her more afraid for me. Afraid *of* me." He looked at her again, his expression hardening, despite the glassy haze of the alcohol. He refilled his glass and topped hers off. "I'm sure she was happy to see me leave."

"Why are you here?" Erin asked.

"I've got a work conference going all week at the Fairmont."

"Then why aren't you there?"

"People just drink there. They brag there. It's no place for me now."

"None of the articles ever said your name," she said.

"What?"

"The articles about the robbery."

"Oh." His fingers clenched the glass, but he glanced at the metal skeleton on the mountainside instead of taking a drink. "It's Edward."

"Erin." She reached across the table to touch his hand. He accepted the handshake, but his palm was chilled from the glass. His grasp held hers limply, lifelessly, taking what little warmth Erin had.

He took note of her flinch. "I was never a warm person. That's why I drink, and why I usually do it alone."

He refilled both glasses, and their second drinks turned into third drinks, fourth drinks. Fifth. Some of Edward's reserve gave way in his inebriation, and he told her of the worry that had often settled over his wife every time he returned from work with an open bottle. He spoke of the fear that had grown every time he woke up screaming with limbs shot full of adrenaline. As he spoke, he kept his gaze averted, turned to the window and its view of the lifeless gondola and its red cabins, suspended motionless in the air.

Finally, Erin said, "This whole time, I thought you were dead."

Edward slouched and twisted the cap over the remnants of gin. Then he touched the spot where the bullet had entered him, just over the pocket of his button-down. "I was halfway dead for a while. It wasn't bad, honestly. Comas are just dreams."

"Can I see it?"

Edward hesitated, but she still found herself reaching out. He pushed her away, the quartz ring thudding against the table. "You shouldn't touch me," he said, standing.

Erin remained in her seat. "I'm sorry. I just had to know you were okay."

"You *know* I'm not okay." He rubbed the gunshot wound, scratched at it like there was something inside that he couldn't get out. "You're not okay either, Erin. You wouldn't be here if you were okay."

She stood. She stared at him, then found herself drawing closer to him. He caught her and stumbled himself, his back hitting the closet door. It rattled, but what she felt was the warmth of Edward's breath hitting her neck.

"Please. Please," he said. Begged.

Erin kissed him, grit on his lips. At first, he resisted, but she buried her tongue in his mouth. He still smelled of gin. His tongue burned of it. Her lungs took full breaths of his hesitant moan.

Life. Friction. Warmth.

His chest throbbed beneath her palm. She pulled at the buttons of his shirt, but his warmth faded as he pushed her away. She stepped back, replacing his presence with what little relief she could get. Teeth to the quartz, she felt the vibrations. The tension. She swallowed, just like him.

"I have a meeting tomorrow morning. A presentation." His voice softened as he felt behind him and tugged at the suit in the closet. "I don't do so well with presentations. It takes a while to pretend, and I can't pretend if I spend any more time with you." The suit swung on the hanger, squeaking over the metal bar.

"I'm sorry," she said again.

"You're not sorry. You're worried."

She backed away and stood hopelessly in the center of the room, giving him a moment to steel himself.

Instead, he picked her parka off the bed. Then he went to the table and took the near-empty bottle of gin. "You'll be sorry if you come back here," he said, pushing the items into her hands. "This will help you more than I can. Just drink. Forget."

The clear liquid sloshed in the bottle after he shut the door in her face.

> Did you get there? You never messaged me.
> I'm worried.

Erin didn't answer her fiancé when she woke up the next morning. She drank the rest of the gin, pulled her parka back on, and left her room. She pressed her ear to Edward's door, but he was no longer inside. She imagined him standing before a crowd of people in his pressed gray suit, imagined his voice shaking before them—unlike when he spoke to her, hard and authoritative and affirming.

It wasn't until she returned to the village stroll that she realized she'd forgotten her gloves again. Everyone around her had thick insulated ones, which they used to carry their skis casually over their shoulders. Erin lowered her head and wove between them for the nearest cafe. She took it in a paper cup this time, then clutched at it as she lined up to ride the gondola. Thirty bucks admitted her into one of the red cabins with a glass floor. The door sealed shut. The lift started. The ground drifted from her feet, and the lift carried her up the mountain, high above all the people and trees and lakes expanding below.

Halfway up, the doors rattled, and a draft slipped through the gap. Erin stared at the misaligned panels and took a sip of her coffee, hoping it would warm her, but all she felt was the grinds against her teeth. She set the cup on the floor and sat on the bench, staring at the peaks of the snow-covered cedars drifting below.

The cold quickly found her extremities, her fingers and her cheeks. She curled her toes in the confines of her leather boots. Tension worked through her. She hated the way the cabin swayed in the wind. Her rib cage tightened around her lungs. She struggled to draw a breath, closing her eyes only to picture Edward lying on the glass floor, the view of the mountainside filling with his alcohol-thinned blood.

A gust of wind rattled the doors and parted them further.

She shivered as the cabin neared the mountain's peak. The sky turned black and endless, but the people gathered at the top of the mountain didn't seem to notice. They put on snowshoes and roasted marshmallows, bonfires licking at their extended hands. The red cabin stopped at the peak's landing, but the broken doors refused to open.

Erin clawed at the doors for the fire's warmth, only for her bare fingers to turn black against the dry mountaintop air. She shouted for help. Nobody turned. Nobody saw. Then the gondola started again. It carried them back down the mountain, where the sky brightened but didn't clear, trapped in a perpetual state of gray. Trees poked out of the snow. Black dots turned into skiers who knew how to stop at the bottom of the hill.

At the bottom, Erin pounded on the doors. They opened and she scrambled out of the gondola, knocking over her coffee. She left the spill and retreated to the hotel, the sting of frostbite seeping through her unprotected fingers.

The elevator buttons felt like nothing. Every digit screamed, her fingers turning red and swollen in the hotel's warmth. She tried to retrieve her room key, but the flimsy plastic slipped from her useless grasp. She moaned, curling her frozen fingers into her frozen palms. The ache swelled through her hands, up her wrists and into her forearms.

The elevator doors parted, but she passed her room and pounded her fists against Edward's door.

"Please!" she cried. "Please!"

The door fell open. "Let me see," Edward said. He grabbed her hands and gawked at the blackened swelling.

"I forgot my gloves."

"Where did you go?" he asked.

"The gondola. I just wanted to be normal. I wanted to see."

He pulled her up and exhaled with concern.

"T-they're going to have to amputate them, right?"

"No," he said, dragging her back to his room.

His hands weren't much warmer in front of the fireplace, but he massaged her palms, pressed his fingers between

hers. Friction. Tension. The electric flames still created something before them. Her heart started pounding. Then Edward twisted the quartz ring off her left hand.

"My wife loves this kind of shit."

"It doesn't work," she admitted.

"Of course, it doesn't. It's a fucking rock." He set it on the
nightstand and replaced it with his interlocked fingers, digits
pressing between her knuckles, palm pressed to the back of
her hand. He turned the frostbite red, then white, then pink.
The pain turned to pins and needles. The swelling disap-
peared. Sensation returned and gave way, finally, to his
warmth. Erin curled her grasp into his and squeezed tightly.

Despite wanting to, she didn't kiss him. She rested her
head on his shoulder, and they watched the simulated
flames dance behind the glass. Edward drew a breath in the
tension but wrapped an arm around her waist and pulled
her closer. He lifted his hand and tilted her head to kiss her
lips. This time, when she went to touch his beating heart, he
didn't protest.

Piece by piece, they removed clothing, exposing flesh to
the growing heat. Erin pushed him onto the bed and straddled him. She worked herself over him, working her need
over his erection until she found release.

He held her, breaths unchanged and steady, so Erin continued, hoping to do the same for him.

She tried to please him, her back arched, her thighs
aching. She writhed until she was exhausted, and tears
rolled hot down her cheeks.

Edward reached up and wiped them away. "It's fine. It's
not your fault. Nobody can satisfy me anymore."

Night fell, and the white lights in the trees lit the pathways
again. Tourists traded in their skis for shots and debauchery.
Their shouts rose and reached through Edward's hotel window, waking Erin. The pretend flames twisted and contorted, illuminating the room with warm tones of amber and

red and yellow. They flickered over Edward's bullet wound —just a circle of pale scar tissue over his heart. She touched it again, barely able to feel its beat.

Then Edward's phone rang. He gasped and flailed, grabbing for the device to turn off the alarm.

"What is it?" Erin asked.

"It's cocktail hour at the conference." He placed the phone back on the nightstand. "I'm not going." He pulled her closer and took her hand. He tried to get a look at her fingertips, but she touched his scar instead.

"How long did it take to heal?"

"It doesn't always look like that. It's never healed. Not entirely." The flames illuminated his face. He turned toward the red glow. "I should have died."

"I'm glad you didn't." Erin tried to touch the wound again, but he grabbed her hand.

He flattened her palm, studied her fingertips, and squeezed until they turned red. "I won't be able to fix you. I'll just make things worse, eventually."

Erin hesitated, but he brought her hand to his chest again. The scar tissue blackened beneath her touch, the skin thinning as his heartbeat accelerated. Her fingers curled and sank into the cold blackness swelling from beneath the wound. Her nails scraped ribs, scraped muscle, skimming the edge of his heart.

Edward groaned, but he clutched at Erin's wrist before she could pull away, the dead affirmation of his voice finally giving way to a moan.

Her fingers burned, but she buried them deeper, closing her eyes as she leaned over him. She kissed him. She tasted him, feeling the vibration of his cry in her lungs. His heart throbbed, and she prodded at the life still inside him until he cried out.

"Please! Please!" He looked as he had on the tiled floor of the liquor store. She kissed him, promising that everything would be okay, his moans vibrating hot against her neck.

He kissed her, bit at her, the wound turning cold around her hand. Erin flinched and pulled away, only for the black hole to fill with ice. He gasped, flinching as it melted, spilling blue sludge down his chest and onto the sheets.

———

She spent the night and found the quartz ring gone in the morning. Slipped under the bed, probably. Instead of looking, she went to turn on the little coffee pot in the corner of his room.

"We should go out," Edward said.

They shared a plate of pancakes in front of the bistro window. He was still nervous in public. The metal fork slipped in his grasp, and she nudged his foot beneath the table. He forced a smile, forced normalcy.

Afterward, they clutched each other's gloved hands on the village stroll, so all the people with their skis had to step aside to let them through. The sleeves of their parkas rustled as they walked the entirety of the stroll and back. The afternoon light came and went. They had lunch and investigated the sights. They stood at the bottom of the mountain and watched people plummet, their faces red and smiles wide, arms raised in victory.

Edward's phone rang. He pulled it out but quickly tucked it away. "Let's get some gin," he said, putting his arm through hers. The lights on the trees came on, and he led her through the darkening concrete paths to the liquor store.

Erin froze.

"It's fine," Edward said, tugging her through the melted snow at the doors.

She gripped his hand as he led her to the back where the spirits were. He picked a bottle of gin from the shelf.

She looked into his eyes, but he was once again cold, rigid.

He touched his chest through his jacket, his gaze hardening.

She tried to take his hand, but he moved quickly toward the till as if trying to outrun reality. She hurried to follow him. He paid with credit, his fingers turning black as he held the card over the machine.

His alarm went off to prepare him for whatever confer-ence event he needed to dress for. This time, he shut the phone off entirely and led her past the sliding doors, through the sludge, back outside.

Despite the gloves, Erin's fingers grew cold again. "Can we go back to your room?" she asked.

To her relief, he nodded and took her hand.

———

They shared the taste of juniper and pine as night fell. Black seeped through the windows, and they left the curtains open, creating warmth through friction. She wrapped her thighs around his hips and took the cold of him inside of her. Whatever heat they made would be temporary. She coiled her black fingers into his hair, breathed his name, her teeth grating.

The windows fogged.

When it was over, she pressed her ear to his chest, lis-tening to the faint beat of his heart, telling herself that it was louder, maybe faster.

He fell asleep, and she wrapped herself around him, clinging like he was a hostage she needed to keep alive. The fog from the windows faded, exposing the mountainside, still bright with spotlights. The skeletal frames of the gon-dola climbed the mountain like stitches, and the little red cars swayed in the frigid northern breeze.

Erin looked at Edward, his eyes closed, his chest still rising and falling. Slumber. A coma.

The scar was different.

It was black in the middle and white at the edges. The skin of his entire chest had swelled and reddened. She hesi-tated before reaching out, allowing her numb fingers to again slip into the charred flesh. She pressed her entire fist inside, struggling to find his heart. The beating was nearly non-existent. She clutched at the faintest sign of warmth.

All the lights on the mountainside shattered.

She turned, gathering a breath, only for his frozen hands to snatch her by the neck. Edward slammed her against the mattress. She fought to get free, but his grasp tightened, trapping a scream in her lungs.

"Please! Please!" he screamed. He stared at her, begging like before, terror in dead eyes, a man fighting for life.

Erin couldn't beg. She fought, kicked, pressed her palms against his chest as the room blackened. She wrestled her hand back into the wound. She clutched at sinew and bone but found no warmth. Her eyes swelled. Her tongue protruded. The beating filled her ears.

"Please! Please!" His voice echoed.

A knock vibrated.

His hands left her. The gondola spotlights flickered back on. Edward scrambled from the bed, clutching at his chest. He moved to the door and glanced through the peephole.

"Is everything okay in there, Edward?" a voice called. "You weren't at today's meeting. I just came to check on you."

Erin turned, gasping, clutching her throat.

A fist pounded the door again, and Edward pressed his forehead to the frame, clutching his chest as he looked at Erin with tear-filled eyes.

She tried not to cough, holding her breath in limbo.

"I'm sorry," Edward called. "I'm sorry. I was hungover. I —I, it won't happen again."

"You were screaming—"

"I'm alright, but thank you," Edward gasped, shutting his eyes as though pained by reality. "Thanks for your concern. I'll be there tomorrow."

Footsteps faded away and Erin turned into the cold sheets, using them to stifle her coughs. When she looked back, Edward was on the floor, trying to wring warmth back into his blackened hands.

"Now you know," he said. "This is why I push people away."

Erin hesitated, staring at his bare left hand.

He struggled to stand, pulling at the white robe hanging in the open closet. Blue slush chest quickly soaked the front of the terry cloth, but he went to the bathroom and filled a cup with water. "I'll do it again," he said, handing her the cup. "I always do."

Erin sipped. The cold filled her throat, tightening her limbs. Her fingertips numbed over the plastic, creating condensation.

"Frostbite creates lasting damage," he said. "You don't feel things the way you once did. Eventually, you won't feel anything at all."

She cleared her throat and drank, but the water seemed to freeze, prickling its way down. She looked out at the gondola. All the lights flickered but remained on. She cleared her throat over the ache where his fingers pressed.

"Your survivor's guilt isn't helping you," he said. "You're just reliving it all by staying with me."

She winced at the truth, his words cutting. "I felt responsible. I thought you were dead—"

"I'm just trying to help you, Erin. You at least still feel something, don't you?"

She reached for him, slipped her palm beneath the lapel of his robe. He didn't move this time, but she felt inside and melted a little of the ice that had formed around the wound. Tears brimmed in his eyes, and he blinked them away, the cold slipping from his gaze.

"Do you really want me to go?" she asked.

His chin shook as he drew a breath. "Please stay."

In the morning, Erin woke to the coffee machine's rumble. Edward was already dressed. Not in a suit, as he'd promised his co-worker, but in his winter clothes. He slipped his glasses on and poured coffee into a paper cup. He brought it to her, the glare of his lenses reflecting the gray skies. "I'm not feeling the cafe today."

Erin cleared her throat, still feeling pressure where he'd choked her. She sipped the brew, but it tasted of nothing.

"I'd like to go out. Just us. I'd like to take you for a walk, if I could." He adjusted his glasses, shifting the glare so she could see the gentleness in his eyes.

"Where?"

"Lost Lake. It's a bit of a walk." He got up and gathered her parka, boots, and gloves.

"I don't really hike, Edward."

"You can't spend all your time in the village. Nothing about it is real."

She finished her coffee and glanced out the window, where the red gondolas climbed the mountainside

He helped her into her winter garments, then wrapped a scarf around her neck to hide the bruising he had left.

The coffee's warmth coiled in her stomach as they took the elevator down. They ventured out of the village and into the woods. Edward led her through the maze of paths. The snow was deep and difficult to walk through. Erin gasped, her throat tight and pained. She followed for what felt like forever, trying to step into the footprints left by hikers. The woods seemed to darken around her, and she looked up, hoping to see the red veins of the gondola. As Edward pulled her onward, the trees thickened, their limbs hanging, green needles looped together like nooses.

The footprints in the snow ended, as if the woods had swallowed the tourists whole. The snow crunched beneath her, creating a grinding sensation in her throat. She let go of his hand, and Edward turned.

"I want to go back. My hands are getting cold."

"We're almost there." He reached for her, took her, pulled her on as the trees towered over them. The further they went, the more the cold spread. Wind slipped through the coils of her scarf. Snow crept into the tops of her boots. Her thighs started to itch, to numb. The lack of sensation tingled into a burn. Then she noticed the sign for the lake. A red sticker was pasted over it, reading CLOSED.

Edward slowed. His glasses were fogged over when he

turned. "It's just the concession that's closed. Everything will be covered in snow. Untouched. It'll just be us."

"Edward, please. I'm hungry. I'm cold."

He huffed. "What's the point of coming here if you're not willing to see the wilderness?"

The path loomed ahead, dark and empty. Her scarf tightened around her neck, and she pulled at the layers. "There's nobody there."

"That's the whole point," he said. "Do you really want to be around other people?"

She tugged at the scarf, unable to catch a breath. "Please. I like being with you, but not here. I don't like it here."

"It won't be like this at the end," he promised.

"I'm cold, Edward." Her breath fogged between them. Her voice broke. "I'm scared. I don't want to be alone. Please. Please come back and have a drink with me." She held out of her hand, her gasps fogging the air between them until he finally reached to take it.

In the dark of the crowded bar, he became the man she saw on the first day. His shoulders tensed and his throat bobbed, the ice rattling in the glass he shifted his grasp around. Beside him, the television blared another curling game.

"I never know what they're trying to do," he said, nodding at the screen.

"Neither do I," Erin said. "One day, maybe I'd like to understand the rules."

"Why?"

"So, I can feel normal again. My fiancé loves curling."

Edward finished his drink in one swig, drawing a breath, raising his gaze, only for the lenses of his glasses to reflect the game. One of the players threw a red rock. The two sweepers brushed furiously as the player standing over the rings yelled. The rock spiraled down the ice, granite hitting granite, knocking all the yellow stones out of play. The crowd around them roared, but Edward bowed his head and cowered.

Erin rushed them through the slush in the bar. Their boots slipped in the threshold from warmth to cold, and the wind whipped at them when they emerged. The white lights glowed on the trees, leading the way to the liquor store. She felt less anxious about the space, as she was more worried about Edward and the way his gaze would change once he selected the gin. In her worry, she snatched a bottle before he could. She took it to the till and paid. Instead of putting on her gloves, she twisted the cap outside of the store.

Edward smiled, and they passed the bottle back and forth, a load lightened as they emptied its contents along the village stroll.

The warmth filled them, made them laugh, made the cold less impactful. She dropped her gloves, scarf, and hat, her face turning hot as she ran across the snow-covered cement, forcing him to follow. She laughed, running ahead, taking deep breaths of the northern night air as Edward chased her toward the open pit of an empty fountain. It wasn't running because it was winter, but its pool was filled with fresh snow that he pushed her into. Snow filled her boots. Snow touched her cheek, and he wrestled her down, kissing her with juniper lips beneath the warm glow of the white lights.

"Aren't you cold?" he asked.

She laughed, head spinning. "No. Not at all."

He helped her up but stumbled. It wasn't until she caught herself in the snow that she realized her hands were black and the lights from the trees exposed the frostbite for everyone to see. They started to gawk and gather, but Edward took her hand. They gathered her things and then hurried drunkenly back to his room, but he staggered again in the elevator.

"This is what it's like," he said. "This is how it feels every day."

Erin pulled his arm over her shoulder, struggling to maintain a proper grasp as she helped him into the room and onto the bed. She turned on the fireplace and hastily stripped his clothes, his skin numbing hers. She climbed over him and pressed her frostbitten fingers to the hole slowly taking him away.

"How much longer are you staying?" she gasped.

"Tomorrow's my last day," he said. "I don't want to go back. They're just going to worry."

"Who?"

"Them. My wife. My family."

"I was under the impression—"

"That I left them?" He winced, but Erin pressed her fingers inside, finding a little bit of warmth where his heart was still beating. "They keep hoping that I'll come back, but I never do. Not all the way."

Erin kissed him, then moved lower and pressed her lips to the wound. His icy flesh fused to hers, but she inched her tongue inside of him, breathing her life into him.

He gasped beneath her, reaching for her neck, trying to push her away, but he didn't beg. "You're just a dream," he moaned. "You're a coma."

"I want to help," she said. "I'm just like you. I *know* how to help." Her warmth wove his flesh, turned it pink, flushed, fused together. The glow of pretend fire made him look warm, real.

He took her hands and warmed them. He grasped at her, held her close, like all he wanted in that moment was to keep her and make her stay with him forever, in a dream.

She huddled against his body, doing herself lasting damage.

In the morning, Edward canceled his last conference meeting. Erin struggled to make coffee with the flimsy machine, her fingers still numb and stiff.

"We should see the top of the mountain," he said.

Erin used her teeth to tear open a pack of sugar, feeling the granules in the ridges. "You said I shouldn't go there."

"It won't hurt as much this time," he promised, but he put on his glasses, and all Erin saw was the mountain's glare.

They held each other's bare hands at the gondola lineup, as they paid the fare and climbed into a red cabin. The doors closed, and the cabin ascended. Erin noticed the coffee stain on the glass floor, which blurred the view of the snow-dusted cedar trees shrinking beneath them.

"This is the same car," she said, pointing to the gap between the doors.

A breeze whispered in. Edward dropped her hand to investigate.

"Edward, don't."

He curled his fingers between the gap in the metal.

"Edward, please."

"I'm fine. I'm alright." He wrestled with the doors. They rattled as the car ascended, the locking mechanism finally surrendering to his fight. The doors slid open, slamming against the guard rails. Cold surged into the cabin, but Edward barely flinched when the gust tugged at his open jacket. He leaned against the edge of the opening, glancing down at the trees and the lakes and the trails, all buried beneath a fresh covering of white.

"Edward, get away from there."

He clutched at the frame and leaned out, glancing at the void below. "I bet there's nobody down there."

The white mountainside blinded her. She reached for his arm and tugged him back, only for him to cling to the doorway with his free hand.

"I really wanted to take you there." He looked at her, voice flattening. Deadening. "Imagine what it would feel like if people stopped worrying."

She touched his cheek, but her fingers only numbed. "Just wait until we get to the top, Edward. There's a fire there. It'll be warm."

His glasses reflected the tops of the trees. "Nothing warms me anymore."

"Edward, please." Her eyes burned. Tears slipped, blistering her cheeks.

His limbs tensed when he finally looked at her. "You're worried, aren't you?" His tone settled in her mouth, grating against her teeth.

Erin shook her head, taking a step forward, closer to the open doors than she wanted to be. She tightened her grasp around his arm.

"Come with me," he said, looking her in the eye. "Just stop worrying and come with me."

Her hold eased in trepidation, but he reached for her scarf and pulled its cable knit tight enough to strangle her again.

"Please," he begged, pulling her toward the void. "Please!" His boots skidded. Erin reached for his arm again, desperate to help him, to save him, but his gaze was already too cold. He let her go, his black fingers slipping from the knit of her scarf as he fell back.

She drew a breath to scream, only for his black dot to fade into the mountain's white expanse.

The gondola stopped at the top of the mountain, and Erin stumbled out, crying into the cold.

"Oh my God, your hands!"

"Why don't you have gloves?"

"What happened to you? Let me help you."

A crowd of gawking witnesses crowded her, horrified by her swollen cheeks and her black fingers and her breathless sobs. They grabbed her by the elbows and brought her to the fire, covering her with a metallic blanket that crinkled around her frame. They all wanted to know what had happened, staring with worried eyes as everything inside of her turned slushy and numb, just like he'd warned.

"Please," she begged, closing her eyes, hoping to dream. "Please."

CHAPTER 3
A PATIENT, A GUEST
2017

ORIGINALLY PUBLISHED IN *THE CROW'S QUILL*, ISSUE 06 (DEMONS)

Veronica didn't cry after Finn's death. She went to the morgue to identify her husband's face, which wasn't much of one after the accident.

His head was swollen, eyes bulbous, the flesh of his lips torn away to reveal the toothy grimace of the demon that had been hiding beneath.

Veronica kept his motorcycle jacket. The black leather was stained with his blood, but she put it on after his funeral, threw her suitcase in the car, and drove aimlessly.

She ended up at the asylum or, rather, what used to be the asylum.

Now, it was a luxury hotel. Its two massive towers stood like horns over the red sandstone facade of the central administration building. Two sets of pavilions branched out behind it like outstretched wings. The closest wards that housed the hotel were brightly lit, while the still-abandoned ones stood shadowed with boarded windows.

Veronica carried her suitcase up to the front desk, a woman without a compass checking herself in.

The hotel's interior had been sanitized and painted stark white. Only the polished mahogany of the staircase railing hinted at the ornate features that had once existed. A rug ran the length of the wing leading to her room, its strange blue pattern like chipped layers of pastel paint.

Veronica found her door and pressed her keycard to the lock. Her room used to hold two patients. Maybe even more when the asylum was overfilled with people like her. Now, it contained a queen bed with an upholstered headboard. Everything was gray and muted, stark and soulless. The ceilings expanded high above her like heaven. They echoed every footstep, every breath, every creak of the leather jacket. Veronica forced herself to laugh at her situation, but the voice that echoed back didn't quite sound like hers.

Finn's leather jacket was oversized, the embrace of it like his weight over Veronica's shoulders. She ordered a Devil's Food Cake in the restaurant and chased it with three glasses of sherry. She sat alone until the meal swelled in her stomach, until the demon inside demanded it be purged. She got up, but the sleeve of Finn's jacket caught in the chair's armrest. Veronica stumbled and heard a man laugh behind her.

He stood in a white robe, hair wet like he'd just come from the spa. "You've got a hole," he said, pointing at her chest.

Veronica swallowed, tasting sherry. "It's not my jacket."

"Then why do you have it?"

"It was my husband's."

"He must have had a few demons," the man said.

Veronica touched her heart, unable to recall a time when Finn had ever shared his demons with her. Then the demon in her stomach reminded her she still had a meal to purge. Veronica shook her head, feeling the man's gaze as she rushed up the stairs to her room. She did as the demon demanded, shoving a finger down her throat. She flushed the toilet after, then sat in the gray and muted room, uncomfortable with the sound of her own moans.

The former hospital's chapel was now a spa. The pews had been removed and a long, narrow pool dug like a trough to replace its congregation. Despite being midnight, Veronica's keycard let her in. The lights were off, but the moon shone through the stained-glass window.

The man from the restaurant was there, standing naked in the pool where the altar should have been. The water distorted him from the waist down, but Veronica could still make out his shape.

She slipped out of her robe and into the water beside him. Veronica used to sleep with men like him just to make Finn angry. Then he'd beat her until her demons started to show. He'd bring flowers and apologize after.

"Sometimes I come here just to look at the angels," the man said, pointing at the white-robed figures on the stained glass above.

Veronica waded, keeping her distance. She glanced at his overwhelming girth beneath the water. "My dead husband used to call me his angel, back when he paid attention to me."

"Did he not want to rid himself of his demons?"

Veronica glanced up at the winged figures, their gazes softening from above. "He used to let me wear his jacket on his motorcycle," she confessed. "I liked my demons when I was with him."

"But you don't now, do you?"

She swam toward him and kissed his lips. He drew a breath before kissing her back, his generous erection swelling between her legs. "I've only ever known demons," she said, pulling him from the water before he could tell her whether or not he was one.

She hadn't felt anything in so long. She begged him to push himself inside and her pained groan echoed against the ceiling. She clung to his shoulders as he built momentum. She moaned. Tears fell, but she took him, her limbs shaking, and her nails bared. The pain burrowed through her stomach and penetrated her lungs.

"Tell me to stop," he begged. "All I do is hurt people."

"It feels good," Veronica insisted, tears burning her face as she allowed him to finish. His labored breaths warmed her neck as he sobbed beside her. She listened to the pain, finally feeling less alone.

She thought he would be gone by morning, but he sat in the armchair in his white robe. Finn's jacket was draped over the armrest, and the man pressed his finger to the bloodstained tear in the leather. Veronica rose, only for crippling pain to fill her lower abdomen, gripping tight like barbed wire.

"You said it felt good," he said.

"Well, it hurts now."

"You should have told me to stop."

Veronica tried to stand, but the pain swelled. "I don't usually do what people tell me to."

"Is that why you're here?"

Veronica shifted. "No."

"You shouldn't have come here," he said. "They try to find your demons, but they just cut away pieces of you until it's only the demons left." He touched the jacket again, his face reddening like something was shifting beneath. "Every day, people come and walk. They talk about the demons that still live here."

Veronica clutched at her stomach as the pain shifted upward. "How long have you been here?"

He hesitated, the leather creaking beneath his sweaty palms. He looked down at the jacket instead of maintaining contact with her. "They keep shocking me. They keep trying to fix me. It gets really cold at night."

"Please," Veronica said. "Please don't take my jacket."

"It's not your jacket," he said. Still, he stood and brought it to her.

Veronica noticed the scars on his wrists. Deep ones. The

kind one would make if they were serious, not the silly ones Veronica used to make to get Finn's attention. She reached for the jacket, only for the man to vanish and the room to turn cold around her.

Veronica hobbled toward the mini bar and opened the sherry.

———

She woke in the night, the pain of her bruised cervix lingering. It worked its way up her back like an embrace she wanted to escape. She tightened her robe and struggled out of bed. She took her keycard and wandered aimlessly, the pain of the man's influence slowing her steps before a narrow door.

It looked misplaced and wrong, its brown paint chipping, unlike the rest of the hotel's modern white. She pulled out her keycard and waved it before the lock. It responded with a click. She twisted the knob, revealing a narrow brick hall-way. It was just wide enough to squeeze through and ex-tended past the light bleeding in from behind her. Foolishly, she called into the black, "Are you there?"

The cry that echoed back reminded her a bit of her own.

———

Veronica followed the narrow corridor, the pain in her abdomen keeping her pace cruelly slow as she felt her way along the black space. The door at the end opened into a wing of the abandoned pavilion. The walls were minty green, but the soft pastel still looked moody in the night. Moonlight bled through the dirty glass. Veronica expected to hear something, to feel things brushing at her back, but only darkness loomed behind her as she hobbled.

She realized she hadn't brought Finn's jacket and that, for the first time since his death, she was wandering the un-known on her own, a white wisp, a lost soul. She felt nothing but emptiness in the sparse remnants of the century-old halls, and that alone scared her more than the demon thrashing inside her as she persisted. Each patient door remained open, revealing scattered beds and mattresses. She didn't know where to go, where to look. She expected the man to jump out and laugh at her like Finn had when she'd needed him most.

She walked each floor and climbed the steps until she finally heard the man's sobs behind a closed door. She knocked. The crying eased, and she took a step back, clutching her stomach, fingers sinking through the terrycloth. She thought of all the times she had locked herself in a room and hurt herself, secretly hoping someone would come. Sometimes they did, but they never looked at her with worry or concern. Only fear and anger. Annoyance, even.

Veronica pushed the door open.

The man sat on the bed. He shivered. The window was open, and the moonlight cast a white glow over his frame.

Veronica moved across the room, goosebumps forming even when she touched his shoulder. His skin was warm. Burning.

The man turned, eyes wide. He reached for her embrace, but she seized when she saw the blood spilling down his arms. Beside him on the bed was a shard of glass, long and slender with red coating the sharpened end.

"I forgot the jacket," she said. The mattress was already soaked through, but she found herself sitting beside him.

"I didn't want to hurt anyone." He clutched her hand, spilling blood. "I just want to go home."

She gave in to his need for intimacy, squeezing back instead of resisting.

He drew a breath, only for it to break. "You're not an angel, are you? I really hoped you were."

Veronica shook her head. "I'm no different from you," she said, holding his hand until it went limp. His body slumped over the mattress. In her pain, she collapsed atop his rigid frame, her cries echoing in the emptiness as his warmth slipped away.

She woke in the morning to footsteps and voices. A woman screamed in the doorway. Veronica startled atop the moldy mattress, turning to find a crowd of tourists staring at her in her bloodstained robe.

"You're not supposed to be here," the tour guide said.

Veronica pulled her keycard out of her pocket. "It worked in the door."

"Which door?"

"There—there was a narrow door. There was a long hallway."

The people gawked. Whispered.

"It must be part of the tour," one of them said.

Veronica didn't mention the man, for she knew doing so would only make them speak of the demons he'd left behind.

A guard was called. He escorted her back to her room.

Its lock clicked behind her but, unlike the man, Veronica was able to pack her bag and leave down the grand staircase. Before she did, she took Finn's jacket to the converted chapel. She stood where the altar should have been and threw the torn leather in the water, hoping her pain would provide warmth to another lost soul.

CHAPTER 4
THE LANTERN

2013

ORIGINALLY PUBLISHED IN *THE CROW'S QUILL*, ISSUE 11
(MELANCHOLIA)

Every day, I patrolled the hiking trail with my walkie. Its wooden boardwalk led through a forest of ancient cedars and ended along jagged bluffs overlooking the Pacific.

The nearby resort owners hired me because I was large. They thought my height and broad shoulders would scare away the undesirable people who sometimes camped along the trail. It was for good people, not miserable decaying people.

My beige security uniform made me look like a good person, but inside, I always felt like I was in a state of decay. Most days, I watched the breakers and imagined the beige fabric turning dark as I slipped beneath the waves.

A graveyard in the sea, its depths filled with broken men like me.

My walkie buzzed with the report of a drunk woman wandering the trail. I found her on a bench before the bluffs, with hair like a yellow flame and a star tattoo beside her left eye. She held a bottle of vodka in one hand and a knife in the other. The handle was intricately carved, but it was the dried blood on the blade that drew my attention.

She grinned. "You've got strong-looking arms. I bet you're good at moving things."

The ocean roared, but I couldn't pull my gaze from the red caked beneath her nails. "Is that your blood?" I asked.

"Some of it is." She slid the knife into her boot and stood. The swell broke against the rocks behind her, casting a mist over her mangy locks. She beamed. Her eyes glistened. "I'll show you where the rest of it came from, if you want."

For the first time in a long time, my heartbeat accelerated. It burned in my ears, made my cheeks ruddy. Fired synapses. Expanded my lungs. I wiped a bead of sweat from my forehead before taking her hand.

She showed me the corpse of a man in her motel room, lying face-down on the floor in a dress. "I can't lift him," she said.

I rolled him over to reveal a torso full of blackened holes. She'd painted his lips bright red, put blush on his cheeks and pink shadow on his eyelids. She'd turned his broken gaze into something almost beautiful.

The walkie buzzed in my pocket, but she stopped me from answering it. "I need you to help me," she said.

I bought a tarp from the store across the street and helped her roll the body inside. We cleaned up the blood. Its thickness coated my fingers, and I breathed its warmth, the odor coating the back of my throat. After the sun had set, I helped her carry the body to my truck. Then we drove. I found a place along the trail, a slope in the forest that was quiet and calming. A special place. We dumped the body off the cedar boardwalk.

The man smiled as his head bounced. He slid beneath the brush, hidden under the cover of foliage and towering trees.

"He wasn't a good man," she said.

"No man is a good man."

She bent down and retrieved her knife. She came to me and pressed the tip of the blade against my chest. "Sometimes a woman needs a man." She grinned then, the black of her cavities like tide pools I could find a home in. I imagined climbing inside and clinging tight, just a helpless starfish in an angry sea.

I'd always been large and imposing.

People always saw the things I wasn't. The noble man. The hero. The provider. The weight of expectation was so heavy, weighing me down to my bed.

My doctor gave me pills and told me that I needed to be outside, that I needed a job.

All summer long, I smiled at strangers I passed in the forest. They felt safe, seeing me in my uniform. For a while, the uniform gave me a reason to exist. Then summer ended and the tourists faded. Autumn brought a handful of storm watchers but soon, even they would be gone.

I didn't want to take my pills again.

I had been feeling so well on my own.

The weather worsened, bringing rain, but the lack of tourists didn't stop the chatter about the missing man. He appeared in the paper and on posters around town. He had a family, a house, a dog. Daily, I walked the trail, thinking about how lucky he was to have died happy. Daily, I walked past the bench over the bluffs, but the rain had already washed away the blood.

After my shift, I drove to the motel and knocked on her door.

There were times when she was gone, times when she was screaming, times when her silhouette vibrated behind the curtains, fist tight around the knife. This time, when she opened the door, I finally got to see her without her halo. Her skin was sallow, her eyes sunken, her hair rumpled, but when I entered, her expression changed, her gaze so intense it almost wasn't human. She approached. I didn't back away. She was small and the top of her head touched the burn in my chest. She grunted, sinking into me. Her body felt like a tiny lantern in my embrace.

Then she went to the dresser and brought me a paper bag. "I found this at the thrift store and thought of you."

Inside was a plus-size bridal gown. I blinked and saw the ocean break.

She pulled out her knife and told me to strip so she could dress me. The silk stretched over my shoulders. She couldn't do the zipper up the back, and she laughed, placing the veil over my head.

"Are you going to kill me now?" I asked.

"You wouldn't be any fun to kill." She pushed me backward and climbed on top. She held the knife to my throat, and I groaned like a ship taken by a storm.

I took the dress off in the morning and folded it neatly at the foot of the bed. She had marks on her stomach. Some were self-inflicted, but they didn't hide the stretched lines of flesh between her hips, red stripes where she had once held life.

"Momma," I whispered.

At this she woke, reaching for the knife on the nightstand. She glared, but I still pointed, ready to die if she found offense. She put down the knife instead of changing her expression. "I had two of them," she said. "Daughters."

"Where are they now?" I asked.

"They're better off without me." She sat up and pulled her shirt back on. "I wasn't much of a mother. It never came naturally to me. Feeling doesn't come naturally to me. It only ever comes when I get to have fun."

"I'm a ship lost at sea," I confessed. I put my uniform back on and put the walkie back in my pocket.

"I bet you see a lot of other ships out there," she said.

"Only ships that know where they're going."

She grinned. "Those are the ships I like best."

Seagulls cried out each morning. I watched them fly around the tide pools, looking for easy prey. They split urchins and starfish, pecked at the barnacles and devoured their tender insides. The storm watchers foolishly navigated the rocks. There was a sign there, warning them not to, yet they staggered over the wet stone, trying to get as close as they could to the breakers.

I waved them back, but they pointed their cameras to the swell instead, hoping to steal a violent moment of water meeting land. Waves hammered at the rocks, splashing mist, sending them screaming. Laughing even. Then they wandered back down the trail, unaware of just how close they were to death.

She dressed her next victim in the bridal gown. It didn't fit him.

He swam in it, the bloody train twisting around his legs, making it look like he had a fish's tail. The lipstick she'd put on him was smeared.

She'd gutted him, spread his organs about the bed.

He was so young, his cheeks gaunt, his limbs scabbed. A guppy.

I cleaned his blood while sobbing–for the first time in years, fully sobbing. The emotion raged from inside, tears storming in jealousy.

"You're only upset because I put him in your dress," she said. She shook me, slapped me. Then she stabbed me. Just a slip in the stomach, a pinch. A warning.

I staggered back on the bed, warm blood spilling over my hands.

She lifted the blade and licked it. "You're pathetic," she said. "You're a beached whale."

I shook my head.

"If you weren't so pathetic, you'd help me."

I stood and took a step toward her. I tried to press my

stomach to her blade, but she pulled away. I fell to my knees, crying a whale's moan against her breast.

She dropped the knife, then got me a towel.

"Momma's here. I'll make it better."

Together, we found another place in the forest to hide the body.

"None of these men deserve a death at sea," I said.

The posters bled in the rain, the men fading, the danger simmering.

She couldn't find any more tourists to lure to her room, so she moved from the motel into my little apartment. Over the coming days, the silence swelled her frustration. When she got drunk, she got angry. She buried her knife in the walls, the floor, the table. Her chest heaved as she worked herself into a frenzy, fingers shaking, face red. "This is no fun! I came here to have some fun! I just wanna have fun!"

I gripped her shoulder, wrestling the knife from her hand. Her entire body thrashed in my hold. She pounded at my chest with a wild fury through the night. I bore her rage, wearing her bruises until they faded.

My body ached as I walked the trail. New posters appeared, though they were no longer of the missing men. These ones featured an illustration of her face. I touched the star tattoo, knowing that if they found her, they would find me too.

She drank her vodka and laughed when I brought her the poster. "I really hoped I'd have more fun while I was here," she said, the crack in her voice burning desire in my chest.

I could die happily.

I would do anything.

I bought her a walkie, and we found a channel to make our own. I watched as the bad men traipsed over the jagged rocks in the rain. They snapped their photos and walked back into the forest where she was waiting, dressed in a white parka, the hood raised over her head like a veil. I told her when they were coming, and she took each groom for ruin.

She plunged the knife deep, over and over. The blood coated her, soaked her, stretching her beaming smile wide. She became a lantern, a guiding light that held my attention as the men's screams shook the trees.

A couple found her on the path, laughing, her body drenched with life. They ran, but she didn't give chase. She raised her walkie and asked me to find another man. My feet pounded over the wet boardwalk, but it wasn't long before the police came. They surrounded her on the trail, guns drawn. Blood dripped down her knife. She laughed maniacally as the police wrestled her down.

One more, she'd asked for.

She just wanted one more, and when she grinned at me, I ran.

Police boots hammered the boardwalk like thunder.

A storm.

I tore through the foliage and down to bluffs, all the way to the bench where I'd met her. I scaled the roped fence separating land from sea. I looked to the water. A figure stood beneath the waves, a lantern beckoning. I smiled and jumped, my uniform darkening as I slipped beneath her swell.

She hammered me against the rocks, and I clung, a black star finding home.

CHAPTER 5
A LESSON IN SOPHISTICATION

1982

Harmony came to me a delinquent. Principal Hendricks was certain she was troubled, and I wouldn't be able to do much with her. The teachers talked about how she had lived on a commune and how her socialite mother received custody after her father's death. Stories of her background circulated, isolating her from the other students who wore their uniforms without qualm. Harmony, however, sat in the back of my classroom, shoulders tight beneath her blazer. She consistently pulled at her stiff collar, yet kept her gaze intently focused on my lessons.

I wrote a red F on her first exam.

Please see me at lunch if you want to talk.

Shocked was I, the day she knocked on my classroom door. She dug her test out of her backpack, defiance in her eyes. "I'll be eighteen at the end of the year. Do I really need to know these things?"

"If you'd like to pass the next exam, then yes, you do."

She sighed, her failure as red as her cheeks.

"Pull up a chair," I said. "Let me help you."

Her steps echoed across the mahogany floor, the chair legs scraping. She pulled an apple from her bag and polished it in the pleats of her plaid skirt. She took a bite, the crunch echoing, ambrosial sweetness filling the space between us. "I didn't ask to be here," she said. "My mother forced me to come so I could be *sophisticated*. There's nothing sophisticated about this place."

"You're referring to your classmates?"

"I know the teachers talk about me, too."

I reached for a pencil. "I don't pay much attention to gossip."

She edged her seat closer, her stockinged knee touching mine.

I took a clean copy of the exam and proceeded to work through each equation, her defiance giving way to determination.

She bit into her apple again. A fleck of red skin stuck to her lip, and she licked it.

My throat bobbed, then tightened. I shifted in my chair, wiping the sweat from my brow before returning to the test. "You know, I grew up on a farm. I was homeschooled for a while. I didn't want to come to the city, either."

She scoffed. "You wear old cashmere sweaters over dress shirts. You look like you've gone to private school your entire life."

I picked at one of the moth holes, knowing she'd noticed it. "Perhaps that's my intention. Being *sophisticated* isn't so hard."

"Sophistication shouldn't be so important," she said. "Love is more important. Community is more important. My father taught me that."

"I don't disagree," I said, my voice soft, hesitating. "The math I'm teaching is practical, however. See, in this question, you're figuring out how much you'll need to budget every month for an Upper East Side apartment."

"I never planned on working in the first place. Once I turn 18, I'm going back to the commune."

"Please, Harmony. You just need to finish twelfth grade and you can do whatever you want."

She sighed and returned to the problem. She finished it under my scrutiny, her face contorted at the true reality of what it meant to live comfortably, to afford a home, have a couple of kids in the city. Things I myself didn't even have.

She wrote her answer on the page. "Now I know why my mom married my asshole stepfather when she got here."

I lifted a hand, wanting to touch her shoulder and give her proper praise.

She looked at me as though expecting it, her eyes glassy. Begging.

I curled my fingers over her blazer, massaging at the tension lingering there. "You've done wonderful work, Harmony."

"My father used to tell me that, too," she said, smiling with flushed cheeks.

In the staff room, the other teachers sometimes spoke of Harmony.

"Her commune was a cult, I'm sure of it."

"I'm certain there was abuse on that farm."

"Before school, I entered one of the washrooms and caught her picking scabs off her arm."

I ate my ham and cheese sandwich in the corner, forcing myself to speak up. "She actually came to me yesterday, asking for help. She'll do well here with some extra attention."

They all smirked, straightening in their seats.

Principal Hendricks shook his head. "Honestly, Mason, you're better off letting her slip through the cracks. Her presence here is bad enough, and we definitely don't need her name appearing on any honorary lists."

I nodded in obligation, sophisticated enough to agree.

Harmony moved to the front of the class, her dark hair the only thing I could focus on when winter came, and frost filled the windows. Students often brought their wool coats to class, as my room was located in one of the school's old and neglected wings. Shocked was I, the day Harmony entered in a worn, fur-lined jacket with a homemade pie in her hands and devotion in her eyes. It was an apple pie. It had no crust, and I gasped at the exposed filling. It glistened with thinly cut apple slices that she'd neatly rolled and arranged so the red skin resembled a garden full of tiny roses.

My throat tightened. "Did you make this, Harmony?"

"It's a rose apple pie. I used to make them on the...the farm."

Whispers started.

"It's so ornate, Harmony. It's absolutely beautiful."

Harmony smiled, her cheeks again flushed.

The whispers rushed about the room like the cold breeze beyond the window, so I moved to the blackboard and picked up my chalk. I taught, feeling her eyes on my back. I imagined the taste of the pie on my tongue. Everything blurred and I adjusted my glasses, turning to the class only to see Harmony in the foreground, hers the only hand raised in a sea of sophistication.

I set the pie in the staff room, hoping the other teachers might taste it and find faith in her. It still sat untouched at the end of the day, so I covered it and took it home. I did my grading in silence as the pie heated in the oven, its sweet smell slowly filling the cold bachelor apartment with warmth.

I gave Harmony a C+.

You've shown such promise. I'm so proud, Harmony.

I sliced the first piece carefully, trimming around the little roses so as not to sever them. The pie tasted just as it looked. Sweet. Spicy. I bit into its dark streaks, which held the strong taste of cider. The crust was tender, the crisp gentle beneath my bite. I served myself a second slice, followed by a third, and then my indulgence reigned, and I consumed the entire dish. I licked at my lips, licked at my fingers, licked at the remains on the aluminum plate until I tasted blood.

As winter froze, she brought me tarts, pastries, and other confections, which the other students often snickered over, their whispers slipping into the ornate hallways.

I marked Harmony's next test with a B.

Please stay at your desk after class.

When the bell rang, she sat waiting, her smile light and her gaze bright. I placed the crumble she'd brought me on her desk, already tasting the morsels of sugar against my tongue. "Don't you worry about what your classmates say when you give me these?"

"I already hear them in the hallways. They call me Teacher's Pet. I don't care what they think."

I swallowed hard, holding sophistication down.

"I make my pastries in gratitude, Mr. Blakely. Did you enjoy them?" She stood, and I backed away a little, noticing the frost that now covered all the windows, isolating us from the world. I stumbled and she took my wrist.

For a moment, it felt warm, her grasp wrenching me to look at her, to address her. It was wrong to admit that intimacy was all I really craved. I wanted her smile, wanted her validation, and I softened under her pleading expression.

"Truthfully, Harmony, I devoured them. I savored every bite." I bowed my head, near tears, glasses slipping. She caught them before they could fall.

"I've heard the things they say about you, Mr. Blakely," she said, pushing the lenses up my nose, allowing me to see. "They make fun of your sweaters."

"Of course, they do."

She helped me to my chair, the hem of her skirt skimming my knee. I caught my breath and shifted my leg, raising the wool to reveal the streak of red on her outer thigh. It was a mottled scar, its initial slit scabbed and swelling over with a purpled crust in various stages of healing.

"There used to be a wooden fence surrounding the commune," she said. "When my mother left, she tried to take me with her, but I managed to get away. I scratched my leg climbing the fence, but I still managed to stay on the farm. It was all I knew. Then Mom came back with papers." She picked at the red line. Blood slipped from the scab.

"Why do you do that?" I asked. "Does it make you think of your daddy?"

Her brows furrowed. "I didn't call my father *Daddy*."

"Some of the girls here do," I said, unable to keep myself from reaching out, from touching ambrosia.

I stopped bringing lunch, as my stomach always ached when the other teachers spoke of Harmony in the staff room. I graded papers, always tasting the ripped fruit.

"I always wonder where she gets her apples."

"Maybe she conjures them. Maybe they were Satanists."

"I doubt devil worshipers would give their daughter a ridiculous name like 'Harmony'."

"She makes you desserts, doesn't she, Mason?"

I clicked at my pen and raised my head. "She's actually quite skilled. She could open a bakery if she wanted to."

You're the only good person here, Harmony.

Everyone looked, faces twisted in doubt. Mockery.

Principal Hendricks filled his coffee from the machine and laughed. "Honestly, Mason, she was in a cult. Best you devote your time to your real students instead of that little barn hippie."

I bit the end of my pen because I was foolish enough to protest. It burst in my mouth, the red spilling, staining the knit of my best sweater.

Winter's end brought perpetual rain, the humidity fogging the windows of my empty classroom. I finished marking the semester's final exams, only for Harmony to enter with a hand-knit sweater in her hands and desire in her eyes.

I dug through the finished tests for hers, marked with an A-.

You're such a delight, Harmony.

On the first day of spring break, I replaced my cashmere with her hand-woven wool. She came with a bag of apples to the empty school and taught me how to slice them thinly. It took me a while to learn. I cut my fingers. She scratched at her scars, and we bathed the slices in lemon juice, acidity stinging our wounds. We arranged the slices, red skin exposed in a white dish. She poured boiled cider over the roses. When the final bell rang, I pulled my car behind the school and she climbed inside, the pie on her lap, ready for warmth.

———

Spring brought buds. They swelled on naked branches, puckering pink as the days counted toward graduation. Soon, she would be eighteen. Soon, she could do whatever she wanted. The sun rose and heated my classroom. In every period, Harmony picked at her scars until red ran down her legs. Whispers sounded and I'd look, hers the only hand raised in a sea of accusation.

Her last exam, I finally marked with an A+.

Daddy's so proud of you, Harmony.

Pride meant nothing, however, when Harmony and I walked to my car with a freshly prepared pie, only to find Principal Hendricks waiting. The police were there alongside her mother. Harmony took my hand. My hard-soled shoes scraped over the pavement, but she rushed through the parking lot and off the school grounds. She pulled me into the woods as the police gave chase, all their voices calling me a fool, a pervert, a horrible man.

I ran until my shoes slipped in the mud, falling face-first into a puddle that tasted not of ambrosia, but of bitter red ink.

CHAPTER 6

HONEYMOON
1979

The moon was full on your honeymoon. It's still full now, its white light pressing through the trees surrounding your little villa. The room's mirrored ceiling reflects the woman you always aspired to be, sprawled on the heart-shaped bed in your blue peignoir set, nipples erect against the sheer nylon. Your long copper curls coil between the pillows. Your legs are parted, and your arms are splayed above you, eyes swollen and crusted with tears.

You close your eyes to shield yourself from the shame, but moonlight pushes through the open curtains. Its perfect circle looks like a peephole carved into the sky. Outside, the trees shift in the night breeze, their branches like hands with weary fingers trying to wave. You blink. A shadow moves beyond the window. A human figure, approaching.

You scramble off the bed to close the window and feel for the light switch, bathing the room in a kinder light. A warmer light. The villa's carpeted walls cushion the sound of the heart-shaped tub filling to your right. It's surrounded by mirrors, reflecting the red embers in the cone fireplace centered in the room.

"Curtis?" The carpet silences your call like a padded cell. You look up and find yourself in the ceiling again. The mirror distorts reality, makes it seem like you're looking down on yourself. You rub the dried tears from your eyes and wonder whether you are indeed crazy. The official at the courthouse sure looked at you as though you were, marrying a man nearly twice your age.

"I'm going to take care of you, Darlene."

That was the last thing Curtis said to you, wasn't it?

You remember him saying those words before he kissed you as his bride, his lips tasting of Pepsi. Your heart pounded then. It starts pounding again, the memory a trigger, bringing you back.

The tub overflows, water trickling between red tiles and spilling over the carpeted platform. The thick-piled shag swells with moisture. You run for the faucet. It squeaks. The water stills, leaving you alone with the sound of bubbles popping.

Wet, like footsteps slapping over the carpet.

You turn and stumble over the fire poker lying before the cone hearth. You reach down to pick it up, spotting a set of wet, black footprints buried in the thick pile. They trace across the room and to the door.

You raise your eyes, only for the moon to find you again. The curtains are wide open. A shadow moves off the doorstep and to the window for a better view.

"No, please," you beg.

The shadow is faceless, and it raises a Polaroid camera, forcing you to shield your eyes from the flash.

Remember how all this started, Darlene?

You didn't apply for college, and your father wasn't pleased. He used to have such high expectations of you, but then you graduated and tried to escape those expectations by joining a commune. You washed clothes in giant batches, fried freshly laid eggs over a fire, and fucked with abandon. It was the life your mother probably always dreamed of, but it was the absolute lack of expectations that sent you crawling back home.

A normal father would have expected you to find a husband and live a normal life, but yours was different. He didn't want you turning out like your mother, so he got you an apartment. After a year of rent-free living, he demanded you get a job. You said you couldn't do that without a car, so he gave you money to buy one.

That was how you found yourself wandering the lot of a used car dealership, eying a yellow 1975 Ford Escort. The salesman came out of the shop holding a bottle of Pepsi. Condensation dripped down the curved glass and onto his fingers. He smiled with his approach. You returned it in earnest, despite being put off by his appearance. His outfit was too coordinated. The warm tones of his yellow dress shirt matched his tie. His brown shoes matched his brown belt, and its gold buckle matched his aviator glasses. Even his name tag matched—cream-colored plastic with brown embossed lettering.

CURTIS

You laughed to yourself, wondering whether he'd purchased his entire ensemble from a single page of the Sears catalog. Still, you liked the way his neck bulged against his collar when he swallowed the dregs of his Pepsi. He pulled a pair of keys from his pocket and held them up, the metal jangling. "You looking for a new ride, ma'am?"

You blushed. *Ma'am.* The term didn't make you feel old, just older. You liked feeling older for once. You liked that he made you feel like a 25-year-old woman, not some irresponsible little girl buying a car with her daddy's money.

You nodded at the car, even though the price scrawled on the windshield was well above what you had in your purse.

"This one's only four years old. Lots of mileage left." He traced his fingertips over the hood before focusing on you. "It matches your eyes."

Your tongue swelled. You pressed it to the roof of your mouth, suddenly overwhelmed by thirst.

He unlocked the driver's door and held it open the way a servant might for a proper lady.

You slid into the driver's seat, hand accidentally hitting the polished knob of the gearshift. "Shit. It's manual."

He leaned over the open door and laughed. "You don't know how to drive a manual?"

"No," you said, your voice wavering. "My dad never had the time to teach me. My mom wanted to, but she didn't have her license for very long."

His brows furrowed. "Oh."

"It would have been perfect if it were an automatic."

Curtis shrugged. "It's never too late to learn."

Your grasp shifted over the wheel. "This one's out of my budget, anyway—"

"Those numbers don't mean anything. And, if you'd like to take it for a drive, maybe I'll give you a discount."

He was close enough that you could smell the Pepsi on his breath. His paisley tie dangled between you, its knot bobbing when his grasp tightened around his drink. He licked his lips, but the bottle was empty.

He was thirsty, just like you.

You took him up on his offer, and he climbed into the passenger seat. He handed you the keys and your fingers touched. They tingled. Then you started the car. Its engine purred through you, in your lungs and between your legs. He nodded at the gearshift, but you didn't take it, not right away. You held your clenched fist at your side, knuckles shifting, taking too long.

"Take a deep breath," he said, moving his hand over yours. "Don't stress. It's not a big deal. You can do this. You're a big girl." He pressed his fingers between your knuckles, working your hand open over the gearshift. His hands were big. His palms were clammy. He had a wedding ring, but that wasn't going to stop you.

He took you around the block and told you how to press the clutch, how to grip the stick and shift gears. When the engine revved, you felt it inside you, like it was jostling all your broken pieces to where they needed to be.

You gasp and wake in darkness, only to find yourself seated at the heart-shaped bar of the resort's nightclub. This is exactly like the first night you got here, but it isn't really like the first night you were here, because the nightclub is empty and there's no music. An empty martini glass rests before you on the dust-covered bar. Curtis sits beside you.

You try to reach for your glass, even though there is nothing inside. You still have an instinct for distraction. A muscle memory for a good time. There's nothing to distract you when he grabs your hand. He pulls you close, his laugh vibrating in your ear like an engine. "Should we go back to the villa, Darling?"

An ache fills your lungs as you survey the dilapidated nightclub, its gold curtains and mahogany walls. The people in the murals all look at you, their faces distorted and their eyes white like full moons.

"I want to go home," you say.

"You can try, but you won't make it. There's no way back."

The vinyl stool sticks to the back of your thighs, but you peel yourself away. In the silence, you hear footsteps echoing. They don't come from inside the nightclub, but beyond the closed double doors.

Curtis catches you by the wrist, his voice firm against your ear. "They can't help you."

You struggle, but he twists you back against him, arms encircling you as he pulls you over his lap. It's not as comfortable as you remember. It's cold, sticky.

Footsteps approach from outside the door.

"Who is that?" you ask.

"A trespasser," he says. "They don't know anything about you. They don't know what you become when you're with me."

You falter over his lap, your hand slipping over something hard in his pocket.

He chuckles, his laugh feeling like pin pricks in your lungs. "You wanted to be mine, Darling," he says, slipping a hand between your knees. They still part for him. Even here, you have an instinct for danger.

He puts his feet under your calves to hold them open.

He pulls at your sheer blue robe and curls his fingers under the hem of the negligee beneath. He kisses your neck, slipping his hand past the waistband of your matching blue panties. His glasses scratch your cheek as he presses his lips to your ear. "Open for me, Darling," he says, pinching your folds, flicking your clit.

You fight the sensation, thighs shaking as you part yourself for him, a delicate blossom in his hold.

"You should pose for them," he says, but you shake your head.

You slip your hand over his lap, trying to feel for the object in his pocket, only to touch his erection. He grasps your throat, condensing your moan of pleasure into a whimper.

You arch against him, feet slipping, buttocks sliding against the girth of his desire.

"You used to pose so well for me," he says, his voice hardening as he pulls you up.

The footsteps approach and the door opens, revealing a dark shadow—a tall silhouette holding a camera. You remain still, thighs splayed, gasp echoing in the emptiness.

"You used to love being like this," Curtis says.

A flash goes off and captures you forever.

Remember when Curtis first called you?

"Darlene?" His voice sounded different. It wavered. The confidence from the car lot was gone, and there was a shyness in its depth.

You even heard a kid shouting in the background and knew he was calling from home.

"I just want to know how things are going with the car," he said.

"Isn't it customary to send your customers a card?" you asked, twisting the cord around your fingers. You didn't want to admit that you still struggled with the clutch. You often stalled at intersections, the people behind you honking. "I like it. It suits me."

He laughed against your ear, voice so low and penetrating that you felt like he was in the living room with you, eating leftover Chinese food to yet another rerun of *Bewitched*. He started humming the theme song. "You don't seem like the type of girl who'd spend her Friday nights watching old TV shows."

"I used to watch it with my mom when I was a kid."

Silence fell over the line.

"Is she not around anymore?"

"No," you said, not entirely telling the truth. You straightened in your seat, redirecting focus. "Is your wife not around?"

"What?"

"I can hear your kids in the background. Is your wife not there?"

He cleared his throat. A chair shifted. "My wife's at a Tupperware party."

You heard him take a drink.

"She hosts parties every week. She always leaves me with the kids, but they never really need me for anything. I always end up here in the kitchen, nursing a drink."

You heard his swallow and imagined his throat bobbing.

"I can't stop thinking about the color of your eyes, Darlene."

Hazel eyes weren't that rare, but that the color stuck with him warmed you. You touched your chest and felt your heartbeat quicken.

"Why are you calling me?" you asked.

Ice clinked in his glass again. "I'm bored, Darlene. I get bored sometimes. I get bored a lot, actually. I have nobody to talk to."

"Neither do I," you admitted.

Again, he paused. Silence. "She makes more money than me," he said.

"Who?"

"My wife. She doesn't need me. Sometimes she jokes about leaving me."

You wanted to say that you were sorry, but you weren't. You listened as he shuffled around. The fridge door opened.

He twisted a cap off a soda, the fizz like static over the line. "I started mixing Pepsi with my rum," he said. "Sometimes, I imagine it's what you taste like."

Your heart thudded. "Is that what you want, to taste me?"

He groaned, and you pressed the receiver to your ear, listening to slick friction.

You imagined his big clammy palm in a piston grip over his cock. You imagined the tendons in his neck pressed against the stiff collar of his shirt. You tasted sweetness, sweat trickling down your chest like condensation.

"You can come over and taste me sometime."

The moon was full on your honeymoon. It's still full now, its judgment waking you on the heart-shaped bed again. A knock sounds on the door but this time, the curtains are closed.

You confront your reflection in the mirror again. Again, you're in the blue peignoir set. The fire cracks and you sit up, spotting a pair of footprints on the white shag carpet beside the hearth. The fire poker sits on the floor, its blackened tip coiling smoke.

A noise comes from the bathtub. This time, the faucet isn't running. It's draining and the gurgling water sounds like miserable breaths gasping for air. You tread across the carpet to see a mound of white bubbles piled inside the red porcelain. Something groans beneath. It turns into a deep bellow. An aching moan. You blink and the room darkens, the carpet falling off the walls, revealing black mold. You lean over the tub's edge and the fetid sweetness of the water climbs into your nostrils.

Pressing your fingers into the froth, you reach for what

might be laying underneath, but the doorknob rattles. A fist pounds on the door, followed by a foot. The door shakes on rickety hinges. Another fist. Another kick.

Silence.

You stand, taking cautious steps toward the window. Your heart pounds in your chest as you peek through the gap in the curtains, only for the moonlight to burn a pinpoint hole right into your chest.

Remember the first time you fucked him?

He'd kept calling, saying he'd come when he could sneak away. Then one night, he called from the phone booth outside your apartment, and you brought him in like a stray dog.

He surveyed the state of your little home: the bowl of cereal on the counter, the dead fern beside the window, the dust on the television. He had to move a pile of unfolded laundry before taking a seat on your velvet floral couch.

"It's lived in," he said, his penetrating gaze burrowing into you. It was different now that you were alone. It felt like he was splitting you open, spreading your insides out, like he was getting his fingers mucked up by your viscera. He pushed the laundry further aside, making a space beside him, but you climbed onto his lap instead. You kissed him so hard, his head knocked against the wooden frame of the sofa.

He groaned at first but returned your cry of desperation with one of his own.

You'd been with enough men in your commune days, but he was the first who clung to you like you were sustenance. He stripped your clothing and gripped at your flesh, pinched it, pored over it. You were a perfect object. A perfect thing. You had power in your vulnerability, and you reached for his belt, the metal clinking. You unbuttoned his jeans and freed his erection. You firmed your fingers down the shaft.

"Every night that my wife makes me sleep on the couch, I think of you," he groaned.

You kissed him harder, burying your tongue in his mouth. You straddled his lap. His clammy palms cupped your hips, guiding you over the glistening tip of his cock. Your pussy puckered, blossomed. You pulled him deep into your well.

"I can't eat or sleep anymore. I always imagine drowning in you." His arms flexed, lifting you, lowering you, his drive so strong, he was shaking. "I'm crazy, aren't I? Am I crazy?"

"I know what crazy is," you said, your cunt swelling at the scratch in his voice. He was broken. He had cracks and you'd slipped through. You existed even when you weren't there—a ghost, a specter, a voice in his phone possessing him, luring him from his family and into your sad little apartment. "You're not crazy," you said, your thighs quivering. "You're just like me." You gripped his shoulders, spilling warmth all over his lap.

He dipped his fingers into the puddle and tasted.

"I want to mix you with my rum," he said, laying you back over your laundry. He forced your legs apart and buried his face between. His stubble felt like thorns against your thighs, but you endured, feeling his voice vibrating, trapped forever inside you.

You gasp, finding yourself in the cold of the lobby's phone booth. This is just like the first night you got here, but it isn't really like the first night you were here because, when you call your father for help, his voice sounds off, like a recording.

He sighs. "She's taken a sleeping pill. She was very upset, Darlene. Your whole life, she's been ill, and now she's finally normal, and you aren't here to celebrate. She wanted you here most of all."

You swallow, heart pounding. It sounds like footsteps. A shadow appears on the other side of the phone booth's door.

It's dark and tall and broad, shoulders rising and falling at an even pace.

"Where are you, Darlene?" your father asks.

You clutch the receiver to your ear and sob. You cry for help, but he just blames you for being irresponsible.

"What was so damn important that you missed the most important day of your mother's life?"

The shadow knocks.

"I'm sorry, Dad," you whimper. "I'm on my honeymoon."

Your father sighs. The recording cracks. The line goes dead.

The shadow builds over the flimsy door. It doesn't say anything. It knocks again, stands there. Waits. The wind rustles between the halls like a ghostly cry.

You lift the receiver again, needing to explain yourself. You call back, the rotary dial looking like a silvery moon full of holes.

"We're sorry. The number you have dialed has been disconnected or is not in service at this time."

You dial again.

"We're sorry. The number you have dialed has been disconnected or is not in service at this time."

Again. Again.

A fist pounds on the door, followed by Curtis's voice. "There's no way back, Darlene. Open the door. Let's take a bath."

You remember Curtis finding you, pleading with you to stay. You vow to yourself that you will take his keys and leave but, when you open the door to confront him, you find the faceless shadow waiting with his camera raised.

Remember your novel?

It was just some silly Gothic suspense story, inspired by all the books your mother used to read. She had a collection of cheap paperbacks, and she consumed them like candy whenever your father worked late.

You liked the covers the most. All of them featured a woman in a pretty nightgown, wandering endlessly in the night while a domineering estate stood behind her, a single window lit. In some of them, there was a figure in the window. A shadow. A man.

You used to organize the books with shadows and without shadows, wondering which stories ended happily. There was no way to tell the difference, and your mother just laughed when you asked.

"They all end happily, Darlene."

You didn't have much in common with your mother, who spent more time batting her eyes at fathers on the playground than she ever did entertaining you. But she let you read the books far earlier than she should have. Sometimes she even spent late nights awake with you, gushing over every happy ending. Considering how brooding the men always were, most of the endings felt forced, but you understood what your mother liked about them—she got to be a heroine instead of a woman in a loveless marriage.

You wanted to write a story for her. Instead of applying to colleges your father would approve of, you were writing a novel about a woman who married a brute who still loved her more than anything.

Your mother always liked seeing you working on your typewriter.

"It's good to have dreams," she said.

Dreams weren't practical, though, which was why your father put her in the nuthouse after you'd gone to the commune. You visited her in the hospital when you came back, knowing it was a place you could end up if you fell out of line again. Each time, you sat with her at the table beside the barred window overlooking the parking lot.

"Can you give me a copy of your book when you publish it?" she asked. She was being hopeful, clinging to her only connection to you.

"I don't know if I can," you said. "I haven't had much

time to write." The truth was you wanted to change the ending of your novel. It wasn't one she would have liked, because it took a dark and more realistic turn. "I don't think I could ever get it published anyway."

Your mother looked tired and awful. She got to wear her normal clothes in the hospital, but she didn't get to do her hair or wear makeup. She looked at you, barely the mother you remembered, barely a person at all.

"I'd just like a distraction," she said. "The distractions here are no good, Darlene."

"There aren't any romance books here?" you asked, looking at the sad bookshelf in the corner.

She tucked her hair behind her ear. "Sometimes, one of the night nurses brings her telescope, and we get to look at the moon when it's full. Sometimes, it scares me. Sometimes, it gets so big that the moon doesn't even look like a moon. There isn't even a man in it. There's just an eye, a big eye, and it keeps watching me and waiting for me to do something, but I can't do anything here."

You didn't know what to say. You wondered if the electroshock was really working or if it was just poking holes in her memory. Then a nurse entered the room and told you visiting time was over.

Your mother grabbed your hand. "Don't give up on writing, Darlene. Even if you get a job, you can still have your dream. You can write me a good story. A happy one."

That night, when you got home, you dug your novel out from under the bed. You gave it to Curtis when he came over.

He took it home and called you from work the next evening. "It's me, isn't it?" he asked. "The brute?"

"Yes," you said. It wasn't true, but you liked the idea that he was infatuated enough to connect himself to you in any way he could.

"I'm not much of a brute," he said. "I don't think I could choke you. I don't think I could hurt you. I just want to be with you. I want to spend forever with you."

You twisted the cord around your fingers. "I'd like that too."

The moon was full on your honeymoon. It's still full now, casting shadows of the deer standing before the villa window, eyes bright like copycat moons. You're in the blue peignoir set again, the fabric soaked through with bathwater. The tub overflows onto the carpet. The hearth cracks. The fire poker lies on the floor. This time, the soggy footprints beside it are bloody, and they lead out the open villa door, into the night.

You consider getting up and following them, but the phone on the nightstand rings. It shakes you, jolts you. It rings again, the receiver vibrating over the cradle, begging you to answer.

Follow the footprints or answer the phone? You realize that either option could lead to connection or danger.

The wind whispers to you, but the phone rings a third time, vibrating in your teeth. You reach for the receiver.

"Page sixteen," a voice sobs. Your mother's voice, but it's not a recording. It sounds so real and honest, distilled against your ear. "What happens on page sixteen, Darlene?"

Her words bubble in your throat, tasting like soap.

"Darlene? Darlene, are you there?" Her voice builds into a desperate gasp. "Your father said I'm never going to see you again, Darlene."

Sweat builds over your palms, the receiver slipping as your mother's cries turn into wails, into aching sobs that reach through the line and scratch at your ear.

"Please make the right choice this time, Darlene."

Her voice short-circuits through your hand. Your muscles tense unwillingly, electricity entering your body, seizing your limbs. You fall back and find your reflection in the ceiling, your eyes wide and your sight breaking, eyes rolling into the back of your head until all you see is white.

Remember when you crashed the car?

You were driving back from the hospital, and your headlights glared off a deer's eyes. Two white disks. A flash. A burn. You couldn't step on the brakes in time. Its body slammed into the hood and buried itself there.

You didn't have to call your father because you had Curtis.

He picked you up from the highway gas station and paid for the tow truck that took your car to the junkyard.

You didn't need a new car either, because Curtis started driving you to work when you finally got a job at the convenience store across town. The schedule worked well. You always started in the afternoon.

Curtis picked you up every night at midnight, when he was usually wide awake and thinking of you.

Most nights, you worked with a guy named Ted. He was your age and, like you, he'd chosen not to go to college. He had awful bags under his eyes and often smelled of marijuana, but you didn't mind being stuck behind that tiny counter with him for hours on end. He always read on the job. It was always the same book, a cheap paperback called *The Cave of Time*. He always flipped through the pages at random, going back and forth before tossing it down with a groan of exasperation.

"You should read a different book," you said.

"This is a different book, technically."

"No, it's not."

"It's a *Choose Your Own Adventure* book. 'You're the star of the story!'" he read off the front cover. "'Choose from forty different possible endings!'"

You thought about telling him about your novel, but he didn't seem like the kind of guy who would appreciate gothic suspense. The store was empty, so you let him read *The Cave of Time* aloud. It was written in second person, and it felt almost confrontational to have somebody tell you what you did and how you felt. It felt even worse when you ended up trapped in some kind of cave and were forced to make your first choice.

"'If you seek shelter, turn to page six,'" Ted read. "'If you brave the freezing wind to see more of the world about you, turn to page sixteen.'"

You picked up your fountain soda and drank, the Pepsi inside the cup so sweet and sticky, the syrup ratio wrong.

"Come on, just pick one," Ted said.

Still, you hesitated. "I don't want to make the wrong choice."

"There are no wrong choices. If you die, you just start over." You drank again, but he nudged your shoulder with his elbow. "Seriously, come on. It's actually kinda fun. I've only come across half the endings, and I really want to get to all of them organically."

"Fine." You sighed. "I'll seek shelter."

"Are you sure?" he asked.

You shrugged. "It just feels like the smarter option."

He flipped to page six.

You gasp, finding yourself in the driver's seat of Curtis's Mustang, its headlights revealing the winding road leaving the resort. This is exactly like the first night you got here, but it isn't really like the first night you were here because, when you step on the gas, you feel a cold flicker of electricity. Waves of it trickle down your forehead, and you wipe at the sensation, only to realize your flesh is coated with bubbles from the bath.

The full moon pierces, light bleeding between limbs. You shut your eyes against the glare, but it pierces through, two white approaching moons that you can't step on the brakes fast enough to avoid. The body hits the hood. The metal crumples. The windshield shatters, scattering blue stars over your lap.

Moonlight bears witness to your shame as you feel blindly for the door handle. You stumble beneath the cover of trees. Rocks and brambles cut your bare feet as you rush into the dark. Flat plastic diamonds lie scattered on the earth, making paths through the trees. They're keychains with all the other room numbers, abandoned cabins left to ruin.

What happened to the other people?

Why are you and Curtis the only ones here?

Beneath the glare, you have nowhere to go but Villa #6. The lights are on, but the curtains are closed. You reach for the doorknob, but the door doesn't budge.

"Curtis?" you call, shaking the door to no avail. Only the metronome answers—it ticks in your chest and numbs your fingers. The light flickers, and you spot a crack in the curtains.

Curtis stands naked beside the hearth, hand around his erect cock, gaze focused on you. No smile or sneer. Just a placid stare as he strokes himself. His chest glistens. His mouth gapes. His stomach goes taut as his grasp firms over his desire for you. He takes a step toward the window.

"Please," you say. "Please, no."

Then his eyes roll back into his head, burning white like headlights.

———

Of course, you remember his Polaroid camera.

It was brand new, and he loaded it with a fresh package of film. The first picture he took was of you kneeling between his bare legs, tongue to his cock, licking at the glistening pearl surfacing from the tip. It was thick and sweet, just like the syrup you used to mix in the fountain drinks at the convenience store. You puckered your lips over the head of his shaft, and a flash went off.

The photo slipped to your knees, but he held your chin and guided your mouth back where it belonged. "Give it time to develop," he said.

You gagged, and he took another photo. He told you to hold him at the base, to lick beneath, take breaths, close your eyes, take him in, open your eyes, look at him. Another photo. Another flash. Little squares fell around you.

"Is it big?" he asked. "Tell me, is it big?"

You nodded.

"Is it the biggest one you've ever had?" His voice hardened over the question, but it still wavered, desperate for your answer.

You did all you could to prove it. The end of him prodded at the back of your throat. You held him there and tried not to gag. Your throat constricted. His cock tensed. You fought to hold him, tears burning from your eyes, the room flashing each time your throat constricted, threatening to retch.

He had to put the camera down when he came. He gripped your head with both hands and moaned, spilling syrup into you. It overflowed, the froth spilling past your lips and down your chin.

"Hold still," he said, lifting the camera again.

In the photo, your eyes were white like full moons, and your mouth was wide, lips tilted in rapture, slack-jawed and overflowing like high tide. You looked like you were laughing. You looked crazy.

You felt crazy, cradling that version of yourself in your hand.

Maybe you were crazy. You were your mother's daughter, after all. You started crying, looking at yourself, but then he took your face in his hands and wiped at the burn.

"You make me feel so good, Darlene." He gasped, and you realized he had tears in his eyes as well.

The moon was full on your honeymoon. It's still full now, but you don't turn away this time. You grab the phone and try to call your mother at the hospital, staring at the lingering silhouette of the deer beyond the window.

"We're sorry. The number you have dialed has been disconnected or is not in service at this time."

You dial again. Again. Again.

Curtis pounds on the villa door, his shadow wavering behind the curtains.

"Open the door, Darlene. Let's have a bath."

"We're sorry. The number you have dialed has been disconnected or is not in service at this time."

The phone goes cold in your tight grasp. It gurgles and sucks, sounding like fountain soda spilling into an oversized plastic cup. The line cuts, then throbs. A gush of Pepsi spills from the holes in the mouthpiece. It streams over your chest and onto your lap, soaking your nightgown.

"Open the fucking door, Darlene!"

Curtis's voice deepens. Reverberates. You curl into a ball, retreating into yourself. You lay back and find your reflection in the ceiling, your eyes wide, your nightgown soaked. Crazy.

"Please!" you cry. "Please leave me alone!" You slam your eyes shut, wanting to wake up again, wanting to be anywhere else. Anywhere but here.

The door bursts open. Footsteps approach the bed, and you sob even harder, only for Curtis to pry the sheets away. He's naked again, chest slick with bathwater and eyes red from crying. He picks up the phone and sets it back in the cradle. He leans over your fetal-wrapped frame and eases you back, broad shoulders blocking the glare of the deer. "I just lost control for a moment, Darlene. You hurt me. You really hurt me, and I lost control." He caresses your chin and pulls you closer to the edge of the bed, the taut flesh of his erection stroking your tears. "You won't be like your mother," he promises. He sits on the bed and parts your knees. He leans down between them, his tongue lapping at your well.

All you feel is roses between your thighs. You try to close your legs around him, crushing his ears, his skull, his brains. He turns his head and tries to gather a breath. He writhes, stubble scratching at your tender flesh.

The next time you open your eyes, his face waits above yours—only it's not his face anymore. His eyes roll back. His mouth gapes and a wad of black saliva slips out, landing on your nose.

You stick out your tongue, and he spits again, filling your mouth with thick Pepsi sweetness that seeps from the corners of your mouth.

"You're happy with me, Darlene," he says, his voice a low hum, the threat of electricity. He squeezes your cheeks, molding your lips into a smile as his hands shake with rapture. "I'm going to take care of you, Darling. I promise."

You cough and sputter, imagining your mother splayed out on a hospital bed, gag in her mouth so she wouldn't bite.

———

Remember that time Curtis took you to see your mother?

It was a few weeks after you crashed the car, and he insisted on driving you to the hospital. You insisted he stay in the car.

"I saw you with that man," your mother, her legs restless and bouncing beneath the table. She pointed at the brown Mustang in the parking lot. Cigarette smoke wafted from the open driver's window. "How long have you been seeing him?"

You hesitated. "A while."

"Does your father know?"

"No," you said, finally having something in common with her. She looked at you, wanting details, but you weren't willing to share them. She was your mother, after all.

"I always thought you'd end up with an older man. Sometimes, when I pretend to talk to you, we talk about older men."

"You pretend to talk with me?"

She smiled then; her teeth didn't glisten. She wasn't the mother who always had her hair permed and her clothing pressed. She wasn't the mother who smoked while reading, made cocktails in the middle of the day and was always polite to the repair man who came whenever the dishwasher mysteriously broke.

"Over there," she said, nodding at the trio of phone booths down the hall. "The phones don't dial out unless you have a doctor's permission to make a call, but sometimes I'll hide in there and pretend to talk to you. You tell me about your job and your writing."

"I don't really write anymore," you admitted.

"Why not?"

"Because I don't need to."

She took a moment and squinted out the window. Curtis was older, brooding, a man from her books in real life. "Is he like your father?"

"No. He's more like you, actually."

"How?"

"He's married."

She looked down, then scratched her nails over the table. "I don't know if you should stay with a man like that."

"He's unhappy. His wife doesn't love him. He always smiles when he's with me."

"Sometimes I think of the things I'd do if I wasn't here, and it makes me smile," she said, looking out the window with longing. But her longing shifted quickly into fear.

You hesitated for a moment, looking down at Curtis's silhouette in the driver's seat. You wanted to ask your mother what she meant, but then the nurse came in and announced visiting time was over. You returned to the Mustang but, before you got into the passenger seat, you looked up at the third floor's corner window and saw your mother staring at you, eyes wide with dread.

Another flash widens your eyes. You wake in the driver's seat of Curtis's Mustang, your face over the steering wheel. This is exactly like the first night you got here, but it isn't really like the first night you were here, because there's a body on the hood.

Smoke billows into the night as you scramble from the vehicle, only to find the body isn't a deer, but your mother sprawled on her back in a hospital gown. There's a gag in her mouth and electrodes on her temples, but she breathes calmly, her gaze to the moonlight.

"Mom?" You reach for her shoulder, making contact with hot skin. She starts vibrating, groaning. Her chin bounces and her nails scrape over the hood of the car. Groans sound past the gag. Her body breaks into full convulsions, but her focus remains fastened to the moonlight. Its glare reflects off the tears squeezing past her eyes.

You try to shake her awake, but you only make it worse. Her mouth parts. Bubbles spew past her lips, dripping down her cheeks and onto the car's hood. It's not until you let her go that her moans cease.

Her body eases. Her head rolls to the side, and she meets your gaze, only her eyes are white and glaring. She gathers a breath and says something. It comes out muffled through the gag, sounds like a voice in a phone, the line broken and blurry. You can barely make out your name.

"Darlene! Darling!"

She tries to reach for you, but you back away, her cries too much to bear.

Remember the night Curtis's wife found out?

He picked you up from work and told you she'd found the photos of you he had jammed under the couch cushions. His voice wavered when he told you of the argument they'd had—that she wanted to leave him. All you could do was wonder which photos she saw.

"She said she felt sorry for you," he said, driving to the apartment. "She also said she doesn't want me at home." He laughed, but it sounded wrong. Miserable. Scared.

You said he could stay with you. When you got home, you spent the night watching *Bewitched*, his feet propped up on the coffee table beside yours. You shared takeout Chinese food, but he never laughed when the canned audience did.

Later, he climbed into bed beside you. He lay on his back, and you rode him in reverse.

"You've ruined me," he said. "I'm losing everything, and I don't even care." Emotion took him. His groan gave way to a sob, the sound of his conflict made worse by the desire between your thighs. Your chest burned. Your fingers curled. You worked yourself over his lust until you couldn't any longer, shame coiling into your muscles. They ached so hard you couldn't hold yourself up.

Curtis supported you. His arms encircled your lithe body from beneath. He pulled you back, laid his head on your pillow, and positioned your swollen mound over his mouth. His cock pressed against your lips, and you resisted at first, only to gape your mouth over the warmth. It was hard to concentrate, his tongue lapping you as you tried to suck and not bite. For a while, it felt like crawling. His fingers parted you. His nose caressed your wet clit before he buried his tongue deep between your folds.

Your elbows burned over the covers, but there was power in crawling. You weren't on your back like your mother was when they shocked her. You could get off if you wanted, and you did, your pussy a shower, and his cock a fountain, both of you quenched with each other's shame.

"God, I'm in love with you, Darlene," he said, and you turned to see the smile you put on his face.

You weren't sure if it was what real happiness looked like, but he wrestled you back and kissed you, his body so wracked with emotion that you vibrated in his hold. It made you feel like one of the women on the book covers, eyes permanently wide in shock, in seizure.

His voice hardened with his need. "I fucking love you, Darlene."

He kissed you so hard that you could hear your mother screaming.

The moon was full on your honeymoon. It's still full now, its glare diverted when a camera flashes over you on the heart-shaped bed. The curtains are open. You find your reflection in the mirror, your blue peignoir set in tatters.

"Curtis?"

Movement in the bathroom. The tub's still running. Bubbles froth over the red-tiled heart. They spill onto the carpet, adding moisture to a room already pungent and muggy with heat. Spray-painted on the mirror over the tub are the words: NO WAY BACK.

You scramble off the bed and go for the door. The wind rustles through the leaves, scattering them over the porch. Some of them are white. They're not actually leaves but pictures. Polaroids. One of them gets stuck between the rotted boards of the doorstep, and you bend down to pick it up.

There you are, riding him, the curves of your backside arched, your pussy swollen around his girth, sweat glistening down your back. Your face is turned to look at the lens, but the flash whitens your eyes and makes you look like him.

A ghost.

Remember the night you and Ted finally navigated *The Cave of Time* without dying?

You kept making horrible decisions, and Ted wasn't the kind of guy who let you cheat. Every time you died, he laughed and went right back to the beginning, hoping you'd remember what you'd done the times before and make better choices. It took several nightshifts but, when you finally got a happy ending, you screamed in relief.

Ted beamed. He gave you a high five, and you felt the warmth of happiness. Real happiness. Connection.

Then a flash burned your eyes. Curtis stood on the other side of the counter, camera poised. The photo slid out and landed atop the counter beside the fountain cup full of Pepsi he intended to buy. Ted turned away as the picture bled into the square box, your smile wide and real—the first candid he'd taken where you didn't look haunted.

Curtis leaned over the counter, and the customers looked away. Even Ted looked down at his book, made uncomfortable enough by the moment to escape into fiction.

You reached for the picture, only for Curtis to take it. He slipped it into his pocket. You rang up his Pepsi, and he leaned in a little closer. "I need to borrow your keys."

"Why?"

He shifted, taking a sip. "I need to make a copy."

Behind you, Ted turned the page, venturing back into *The Cave of Time* without you.

You slipped from behind the counter and pulled Curtis aside.

"My wife hired movers. They took all my things to a storage unit. I need to stay with you. I need to live with you."

You turned away, feeling the pressure of Ted's glare against your back.

Curtis took your chin, cupping it between his thumb and forefinger.

"Please, darling," he begged.

Darlene. *Darling.*

There wasn't much of a difference and maybe nobody else noticed but being endeared in public felt strange—felt like you were being called out. Still, you got the keys for him. He kissed you, his lips cold and numbing, but only until he was gone.

You returned to the counter and watched him walk to the car. He got inside and the headlights flickered before the window, bright over your eyes.

"If you seek shelter, turn to page six," Ted read. "If you brave the freezing wind to see more of the world about you, turn to page sixteen."

"Page six," you said.

Ted sighed, flipping to page six. "He's kind of old for you."

"He's not."

"Does he always take pictures of you?"

"Yes."

Ted bit his lip. He kept reading from the book, but it still felt like he was calling you out, forcing you to think twice about what you were getting yourself into.

You awake, holding the key to the villa, standing in the dark of the woods, knowing that Curtis is following you—that he'll catch you eventually. This is exactly like the first night you got here, but it isn't really like the first night you were here, because when you get to the villa, you notice that the top screw holding the 6 to the door is missing.

Now it's a 9.

You imagine your mother strapped to a bed, just like in the movies. She told you that electroshock wasn't at all like that but it's hard for you to imagine her not screaming for help, when really that's all she ever did, throwing herself at any man who'd listen to her tales of woe.

Curtis's footsteps approach, his breaths heaving. "Am I crazy, Darlene?"

It's too late to go back.

There's no way to start over.

There's NO WAY BACK.

"Why do you make me feel like I'm crazy, Darlene?"

Your hurried steps break into a run as you fight back up the trail, the overgrown bushes catching in your hair, branches like fingers pulling at your nightgown, wrestling you to the ground. You scream and you thrash, but then strong, clammy hands grab you. He lifts you in his arms and carries you toward the threshold.

Your husband breathes into your ear. "Let's have a bath, Darling."

A laugh track sounds over you, just like that one that played on the television—the laughter like the wind, like your mother, laughing so hard that she cried.

"You'll feel better after a bath, Darling. You won't regret it at all."

———

Remember the time your mother told you what her procedure was like?

"You have no choice. You bite down on the gag. Sometimes it feels good to bite, to have control, but then it goes black, and you don't remember anything."

You weren't sure why she spoke in second person, why she stared directly at you when she did, but then she saw your fear and averted her eyes, almost as though she was scared she'd revealed too much.

"Sometimes I just go black, and I remember you as a baby, still covered in blood and crying. I remember not knowing if I could take care of you. I remember thinking that I was going to ruin you. Sometimes I think that every time you don't visit, it's because I ruined you."

You shook your head.

"I've just…I've been busy," you said, but then she looked at you like she knew you were spending every night in your apartment with Curtis. You hadn't spoken about him, not since that time you felt concern through her stare.

"They say that if I keep getting better, I might get out soon." She smiled. "I'd like to see your apartment. I'd like to visit you at your job. I want to see the woman you've become." She reached over the table with her thin fingers. "Please be there when they let me out. I wasn't a good mother, and I know that. Please, just be there and give me another chance, Darlene."

You promised, of course.

You promised, but then it all went black.

———

The moon was full on your honeymoon. It's still full, even now that you know better. You wake on the heart-shaped bed. The phone rings on the nightstand. For a moment, you consider answering it as you had before, but the door creaks open. Moonlight spills into the room, revealing the pool of blood on the carpet.

Water gurgles in the tub, where the shadow beneath the bubbles lies. It's no longer running, but draining, the sound of water getting sucked down the hole like a sob. You slip off the bed, drenched in bathwater, hair sticking to your cheeks.

You stare at the darkness before bolting. You run through the woods, toward the resort lobby. The teal room keys litter the floor, from patrons who came and left and probably never lived happily ever after.

You walk past the front desk and up debris-ridden steps. Dead branches and broken glass poke at your feet, but you're too numb to feel now. Polaroids are scattered about the empty hallway above, leading to the nightclub.

You open the door, only to find a pile of photos where you'd once sat with him on that first night. There was so much to do at the resort. You wanted to go swimming and he wanted to go to the gun range. Neither of you could agree, so you both drank instead.

You remember drinking so much that you let him finger you in front of strangers. You liked it at first, a lost woman in a dark room, but then the flashes started.

He called you his Darling Darlene, and he held you like a possession. An object.

The strangers all gawked, shocked and in awe. You remember that feeling of electricity controlling you, that blackness that swallowed you, that cry of your mother finally finding you, coaxing you to run from fantasy.

You back out of the room, out of the memory, and hear yourself crying in one of the closed phone booths further down the hall.

"I don't know what I was thinking…"

Footsteps sound from the hallway leading to the gun range.

"I keep doing things because they feel good…"

You turn to find Curtis naked again, covered in blood

and soap, the camera around his neck, the fire poker in his hand. His chest glistens as his shoulders rise and fall.

"I don't know why I always feel so empty in the end."

He doesn't look at you, but at the phone booth door, gripping his cock in his free hand, stroking it slowly. "Everybody got to see what you did to me, Darling. For a moment, we were happy."

You back away from the door as your sobs erupt on the other side. "I don't know if I was happy," you say, but he doesn't hear you.

Curtis blinks out a tear, but he doesn't wipe it away. He presses his forehead against the phone booth door, keeps stroking himself, his cock hardening over his pain.

"My mom got out of the hospital." You say it but the words don't come out of your mouth. They come from the phone booth. Your sobs sound like a recording. "I forgot all about her because I came here with you."

Curtis grips the fire poker and knocks.

You glance at the dark hallway behind him. It leads to the gun range, graffiti covering the walls. NO WAY BACK.

Curtis pounds on the phone booth. He falters and stumbles against it, his voice breaking. "There's no way back, Darlene! Open the door! Let's have a bath!"

Your cries cease. The phone booth goes quiet.

"We're sorry. The number you have dialed has been disconnected or is not in service at this time."

His eyes roll back into his head, the glare building, spreading.

Then he turns and looks at you, drenched in bathwater, covered in static, his mouth spreading into a grin. "For a moment there, I really wanted to hurt you, Darling."

Another tear slips. It glistens down his cheek as his shoulders expand with a labored breath. He strokes himself to a finish, a white flash filling the room.

Remember the night he picked you up from work but didn't come inside? You clocked out and found him in the parking lot, the passenger seat littered with Polaroids of you and Ted laughing.

"You never laugh like that with me," he said.

"It's not like that," you said. "Stop thinking it's like that."

His grasp tightened over the wheel. "My wife is leaving me. It's almost over. I just have to sign the papers, and it'll be over. You won't have to be a secret anymore."

"Really?"

"Really," he said, and then you sat the rest of the way home in silence.

That night, you sat in bed and tried to edit your manuscript.

He sat beside you and smoked. It was quiet, comfortable. Then he turned and grabbed your throat. He forced you back and pressed his cigarette into your chest. It singed, fizzed, sounded like a bottle of Pepsi being opened.

The cigarette opened you, making a new hole that burned so much you felt your heartbeat racing through the charred skin. You screamed.

He apologized immediately and followed you to the bathroom, where the burn turned white like a full moon.

"I was scared," he said, standing on the threshold. "I didn't mean to hurt you. I just want this to work, Darlene. Please tell me you love me."

"I do," you said, forcing a smile that he was crazy enough to believe.

He walked up behind you, then bent you over the sink, his lips to your ear. "I'm gonna buy you the biggest diamond," he said, clinging so tightly that you felt like he was tearing you apart.

You wake up running. This is exactly like the first night you got here, but it isn't really like the first night you were here, because instead of running back to the villa, you run to the resort lobby, needing to quench your thirst. The entire building is cold and ruined, but you push the door over the broken glass. You steal a bill from the open register, hoping to buy yourself a bottle of water. You find a vending machine, but there's only Pepsi inside.

"I can never go a day without a Pepsi."

You turn around and there he is, your husband. He's clothed this time, wearing the corduroy trousers and the patterned polyester dress shirt and the coat he wore the one and only night you spent here. He nods at your bottle. You twist the cap and take a drink. The carbonation burns in your chest, right where he hurt you.

It spills bubbles from the little hole, and he grins at you. He pulls the bottle from your grasp, tosses it at the lobby desk and takes your hand. At first, you fight, but you've no choice but to follow his lead, crossing the overgrown grounds in your tattered blue peignoir. You don't need a mirror to know that you don't look anything like the protagonists on your mother's paperbacks.

You could scream, maybe fight harder, but there's hardly a point in doing so when there's graffiti sprayed all over the front of your villa.

NO WAY BACK

NO WAY BACK

NO WAY BACK

Curtis pulls you through the moonlight and into the privacy of your room. He closes the curtains and locks the door. Then he sheds his coat and turns around, his gaze changed. He takes you, ravages you with more kisses, more perverted nothings. He moves his hands to your thighs, curls his fingers beneath the hem of your gown. "I've done so much for you," he says, easing you back onto the bed. He combs his fingers down the sweaty ringlets of your hair. "I just want to help you. I don't want you to be lost forever, Darlene. I *need* you here."

His eyes burn red, and you grasp his hardened cock with shaking fingers. He grunts, his body vibrating again. Humming again. Possessed again. "This place could be ours forever," he says, stroking your cheek as he lays you back. He climbs over the pillows and kneels over your face. "I'm going to take care of you, Darling." He leans over your body and presses his cock past your lips, muting your cries before they can start.

You whimper but he buries his face between your knees. He kisses your thighs, thorns prodding, but you give in to the wet drive of his tongue. You buck your hips. You choke. You gag.

This was your favorite position before, but it's different with him on top.

You find your face in the mirror above, wide-eyed between his legs, your bodies tangled in a mutated horror of symbiosis. You try to accept it, but you retch hard on his girth, remembering your mother's confession about how good it felt to bite.

Another flash fills the room and shatters the glass above, your reflection replaced with moonlight. Curtis groans, grinding himself over you, stifling your moans as he fills your mouth with soapy water.

———

Remember the month you forgot to visit your mother? The moon on your chest had waned into a dark patch of skin that itched, and your apartment was littered with discarded Polaroids that featured you in various states of dress and degradation. You didn't bother to pick them up until the day your father knocked on your door, unprompted.

"Just give me a moment!" you cried, but he came in anyway and saw what you were after. He picked the closest photo off the floor. He flinched, and it slipped from shaking fingers, landing with the image facing up—a picture of you kneeling naked with your smile wide and overflowing with gargled Pepsi that Curtis had spat in your face.

Your father blinked, his gaze falling to another image on the floor—you riding Curtis's cock, your back sheened with sweat and your copper hair tossed in abandon.

You snatched the photo, and your dad collapsed atop the dirty laundry on her couch.

"Get me a drink," he said.

All you had in the fridge was Pepsi.

"You are your mother's daughter," he said, his expression altered with carbonation when he drank too much. "You're just like her. I tried everything to prevent it from happening, but now you're even more of a whore than she ever was."

You tried to swallow, but you couldn't, the burn on your chest like an aching mass.

The moon was full on your honeymoon. It's still full now, its bright light revealing you in the tub, head propped up against the point in the middle of the heart.

Your neck burns. Your lungs ache. Your right knee throbs.

There's a hand over your throat, a hand holding you down, a hand cleansing you.

"I'm going to take care of you, Darlene."

It was his vow to you but now, when he says it, it's with malice, his body crumbling over yours, Pepsi spilling from a hole in his chest. He holds you, covers you, prevents you from getting out. You slip into the depths, the dark water shielding your eyes from shame.

Remember the night he gave you the ring? It wasn't big like he'd promised. You didn't really mind all that much, the round diamond glowing like a moon on your finger beneath the dim lights of the restaurant he proposed to you in.

He smiled.

You smiled.

You actually felt happy, felt grown, felt like a person with a future full of promise.

You had that power as a protagonist, after all.

You close your eyes, and everything goes black, a haze of pleasure building between your legs, his stubble scraping at your thighs. This is exactly like the first night you got here, but it isn't really like the first night you were here, because when you try to find yourself in the mirrored ceiling, there's just the moon glaring down like a massive white eye rolled back.

Curtis bucks his hips against your face. His cock fills your mouth like a gag, and you bite down, cutting flesh in your teeth.

You imagine your mother getting better, but Curtis growls in pain.

"You fucking bitch!" He doubles over on the bed, cradling his manhood, blood spilling down his fingers. You remember him moaning for a while and you lying there, feeling judged, feeling like a patient, a woman with every-thing gone wrong.

"I was supposed to see my mother," you say, your mouth tasting like pennies.

He kneels on the floor. His cries go internal, and his body vibrates. Adrenaline. Electricity. You watch from the bed as his muscles tense and his shoulders expand.

"I don't care about your fucking mother," he grunts. Be-hind him, the tub overflows. He picks up the fire poker, using it like a crutch to help himself stand. "You're so afraid of becoming her, but she's not ill, Darling. She just didn't have a real man. She didn't have a good man."

Tears burn down your cheeks.

"I vowed to take care of you," he says, his eyes glazed. His grasp firms over the fire poker and he nods at his coat on the floor. "Look what I got for us," he says. "Your mother won't have to worry about you anymore."

You slip off the bed and reach into the pocket, grasping the cold metal grip of one of the handguns from the shooting range.

He smiles, his eyes going white. "Get in the tub, Darling."

Your heart thunders, aching against your chest. You look toward the door, but he swings the fire poker at your knee before you can run. You crumple to the floor. The gun thuds on the carpet and you scramble toward it. You slip your fingers around the grip, but he strikes you again, knocks you flat, rolls you over and climbs on top.

"Not yet," he says, putting the iron poker across your throat. He pushes down.

You can't go anywhere.

There's NO WAY BACK.

Your arms splay out, useless, the gun flopping over the carpet as clogged breaths burn in your chest. Your limbs tighten. Your muscles spasm, and he stares as you weaken, your eyes aflame with burning tears.

"Let's have a bath, Darling," he says. He pulls the bar away. You draw a breath to scream but your cries go unheard as he lifts you like a withering flower. He picks the gun off the floor, and he carries you over to the edge of the tub. "This is what you wanted," he says, easing you into the hot water. Tears slip down your cheeks and he lifts your hand and places the gun, wraps your fingers around the grip again. You let out a moan and he grabs your throat instead.

"You wanted a brute. You wanted this. I'm your fucking brute, Darling."

You shake your head, but he grabs your wrist and makes you point the gun at his chest.

"I'm going to make you happy," he repeats. "Do it. Do it, Darlene, and I'll make you so fucking happy."

You draw a breath, lungs aching, throat on fire.

He grips your hand. The gun fires, a jolt in your limbs. Your eyes widen and a black moon fills his chest that matches the hole on yours. He falters. He groans. He crumples and lands on you, your neck cracking against the pointed center of the heart-shaped tub. The gun slips from your hand, and you feel for the red-tiled edge, unable to pull yourself free.

"I'm going to take care of you, Darlene," he says, hand to your throat, pushing you beneath the bubbles, stained with the blood spilling from his wound. You try to scream, but your mouth floods with carbonated sweetness. It fills your lungs with sweetness.

You burn in its warmth.

———

Remember how fast the wedding happened?

He came to your apartment after his divorce was finalized. He packed your clothes into a suitcase.

"Finally, Darling," he said, eyes dark with determination. "Finally, we won't have to hide."

You said your vows and kissed awkwardly before the official. Your block heels clicked with your hesitant steps out of the courthouse. Clouds built over the sky as Curtis opened the passenger door of his Mustang. You climbed in beside him, hands clutched tight around the thorns of your hand-picked rose bouquet.

"I got us a villa," he said, jerking the stick shift. He drove too aggressively through a winding highway leading into the Poconos. All your mother's books ended this way, and you hoped you'd be able to smile once you reached your destination.

———

The moon was full on your honeymoon. It's still full now, its circle encompassing the entirety of the sky, its glare reflecting you on the heart-shaped bed. Your hair's arranged neatly over the pillows. You're dressed in your new blue peignoir set, purchased just for the occasion. Your arms are splayed. Your legs are spread, but you don't look like a whore. You're a wife, wanted and needed and loved. You wipe the tears from your eyes and smile.

"Are you awake, Darling?"

You sit up and survey the luxurious villa he booked. The

white carpet is plush. The fireplace cracks with warmth. All your Polaroid photos hang like curtains over the window. You sit up and find your husband waiting in the tub filled with Pepsi.

He smiles as you ease yourself off the edge of the bed, his happiness beaming as you slip out of the peignoir. "You're beautiful, Darling. I'm so lucky to have found you."

You climb into the tub beside him.

He puts his arms around you. "I'm going to take care of you, Darling."

His kisses are sweet. So sweet. Almost artificial. He kisses you with vibrating passion and your teeth feel like they might fall out, but you have to like it.

There's no way to go back. There's no way to start over.

You made all your choices and now here you are.

This is the ending that every woman wants, Darling.

CHAPTER 7
THE WALKING HOURS
1947

ORIGINALLY PUBLISHED IN *THE CROW'S QUILL* – ISSUE 03
(VAMPYRES)

Frederick's neck was itchy when he woke to Julia laughing loudly downstairs. She sounded excited. He scrambled out of bed to find his wife standing in the middle of the darkened living room, carrying a bottle of milk.

"I-I put sugar in, just for you." She held the bottle out, but there was nobody there to take it. The glass shattered against the edge of the coffee table, and she shrieked in delight before kneeling and trying to clean the spill with bare hands.

"Darling?" Frederick rushed over and touched her shoulder. "Julia, you're sleepwalking again."

She lifted her head. "I-I heard a baby!"

"There's no baby," Frederick said. "It's just me, darling. Come to bed."

She wasn't awake, but Frederick helped her upstairs and tucked her in. He cleaned the spill before making himself a bed on the sofa, hoping that he'd wake if she walked again.

Frederick had met Julia in the depths of a nightclub. She was forward and loose in morals, and their necking that evening quickly gave way to Frederick's proposal.

"You're the sweetest man I've ever met," she'd said.

She always wore her red cat-eye sunglasses in the daylight, claiming the sun irritated her eyes. She even wore those glasses in the photo she gifted him before he was deployed to France with a fresh haircut and a gun. The other soldiers gawked at her image, saying if he survived the war, he would be the luckiest man to ever live.

When Frederick returned unscathed, Julia removed her sunglasses on the airport tarmac, her tears spilling red as blood. She nuzzled herself deep in his embrace and flooded his shirt with cries. "You smell just as sweet, baby. Never leave me again."

They married and bought a modest home in the suburbs. Everyone knew he was a soldier, a hero, but Frederick preferred when people commented on the green yard, he painstakingly kept free of weeds. Julia didn't often come outside, as the grass gave her allergies. She opted instead to spend all her summer afternoons in the kitchen, the house always smelling of freshly baked delights when he retired for the evening.

He preferred normalcy, but one night, he woke to Julia laughing maniacally. He had run down the stairs to find her crawling across the living room floor, cackling as she moaned about how thirsty she was. He shook her awake, only for her to thrash and bite his neck, her teeth breaking skin. He knew how to fight, but he didn't fight her. Couldn't fight her, and so he let her lick at the blood as it dribbled from his neck until she fell back to sleep, murmuring of sweetness. Of love. Of strawberry milkshakes.

"I've always been a sleepwalker," she said, serving him French toast the next morning. "I thought I was drinking a strawberry smoothie." She hung her head in shame, but Frederick had tucked his fingers beneath her chin.

"I guess I'm in love with a sleepwalker."

Months passed, and Frederick woke again and again to

Julia stumbling through the house like a toddler, voice slurred and rambling, her dreams fully exposed. He loved her, even if she stripped naked, even if she cursed, even if she spilled drinks and food, even if she opened the door and went for a midnight walk. Sometimes he'd wake to find her gone, and he'd tear through the streets in his slippers, screaming her name until he found her.

He was careful not to wake her, but sometimes she did and found her bearings in his arms. Then she'd laugh. That was her constant. She always managed to make him smile, which was what Frederick did every morning when he walked outside to retrieve the newspaper and the new bottle of milk.

He shielded his eyes from the sunlight, noticing a fresh dandelion poking out of the grass. He stepped off the stoop to pluck it but was distracted by the moving truck pulling up in front of the house across the street.

Out of the truck came a young family: a man, a wife holding a baby, and a boy clutching a toy plane. The boy made plane sounds, bomb sounds, angry sounds. Frederick clutched at the dog tags he hadn't removed since his return from the war. He retreated inside, taking refuge at the kitchen table, where Julia placed a fresh crepe covered in icing sugar.

"It's almost as sweet as you," she said.

He felt the warmth of her smile, but then scratched at the itch on his neck.

"What's wrong, Fred?"

"Just a mosquito bite," he said, picking up his fork.

Frederick spent most of summer's twilight working on the lawn. The mosquitoes sometimes bothered him, but he paid them no mind as he dug weeds from the grass with a screwdriver. Erratic footsteps pattered across the street. Frederick looked up to see the boy from next door. He held the toy plane in one hand and a melting red Popsicle in the other.

"My mom says you're a hero." The boy nodded at the dog tags that had slipped from beneath Frederick's collar.

Frederick crumpled the dandelion in his palm and stood. "Being a hero isn't what they say it is."

"I bet your wife thinks you're a hero," the boy said. "Your wife always goes for walks at night. It's so funny. Once, she knocked on our door and she wasn't wearing anything!"

Frederick tucked the tags back where they belonged. He wiped his forehead, smearing the yellow guts of the dandelion on his face. "She's a sleepwalker," he said. "If you see her, you shouldn't wake her."

"Why do you need to pick them all?" the boy asked, pointing at the crushed petals in his hand.

"They ruin the grass."

He shrugged. "But they make the grass prettier. The bees like them too."

Fredrick wiped his shaking fingers on his leg. "The bees...they sound like the planes."

The boy studied his toy, confused.

"Things don't sound the same when you're a hero," Frederick explained.

"Oh." He went to lick his Popsicle, but the red ice melted off the stick and landed on the grass.

At night, Frederick found Julia standing before the living room window, staring at the neighbor's house. She held a cushion to her face and sniffed. "I-I-I can't help it," she slurred, giggling as she bit into the velvet.

Frederick sat on the couch, but Julia turned and gawked at him. She stood for a moment before approaching carefully, her sleeping gaze trying to make sense of him.

"You're different," she said. "You don't smell as sweet since we moved here." Still, she slipped into his arms and back into slumber.

Later, he woke to find the front door wide open. He

darted outside and stalked the streets until he found her picking up stones in the neighbor's backyard.

"I want a Popsicle, too!" she cried.

Frederick guided her home, trying not to wake her. Before locking the door, he saw the little boy watching from one of the windows. Frederick swallowed and helped Julia upstairs. Then the cries of the neighbor's baby slipped through their open bedroom window.

Julia smiled against his neck. "I want a baby, Fred. Let's have a baby." She curled herself against him and whimpered.

Frederick worked at a factory where he turned nitrogen into fertilizer instead of bombs. He often took home free bags, which he sprinkled over the lawn, hands shaking, hoping the dandelions wouldn't return.

"I finally met the neighbors today," Julia said, serving him meatloaf for dinner. "The mother was nice, but that baby was about the sweetest thing I've ever smelled."

Frederick cut a slice but couldn't coax himself to take a bite.

"You talked to the boy the other day," Julia said.

"Yeah."

"He scared you, Fred. What did he do?"

Frederick shook his head. All he could think of was injured men on the sand, crying for their mothers with their dying breaths. He'd fired his gun over and over, but it was their sobs that rang forever in his ears. He wasn't a hero. He hung his head, but Julia tucked fingers beneath his chin.

"Fred, tell me."

He swallowed. "I know I'm different now. I'm not normal. I'm not like everyone else."

She shook her head. "You'll always be the same where it matters most, Fred." She pressed her hand to his chest, to the heart that throbbed against the metal dog tags. She held them through the thin fabric of his shirt. "You're a hero to me. I can do the same for you, baby."

Fredrick went to scratch his mosquito bite, but Julia stopped him and grinned.

"I made lemon meringue pie for dessert."

Days later, Frederick returned from work to find the boy running through the lawn. He no longer had the plane, just a fistful of dandelions gone to seed. The seeds spilled over his pristine green lawn. The boy still made his plane sounds, his bomb sounds, his joyful sounds.

Frederick slipped back against the car, unable to breathe. Shaking, he felt for the tags that identified him. He clutched the heated metal, hearing gunshots, hearing the ocean, hearing the cries. He closed his eyes and thought of red, of victory, of Julia's lips, her teeth covered with red.

He gasped and tasted salt.

The front door opened. Julia came running, and she grabbed the boy by the ear. "You rotten child!"

The boy flailed and landed on the sidewalk, scraping his knee. Julia wasn't wearing her sunglasses, but she shielded her eyes from the sun and dragged him back toward his house, shoving him at the door. The mother answered and Julia yelled. The boy cried but Frederick just heard the soldiers crying until Julia returned, reviving him with her red smile and red, teary eyes.

"Julia?"

"It's okay," she said, wiping the blood. "Let's get inside. We don't belong out here. It's safer inside. We'll keep the lights out. It's going to be okay."

Inside, she wiped her eyes dry and made him pancakes for dinner. Frederick sat at the table, unable to do anything but scratch the itch on his neck.

"It's okay, baby," she said, rubbing calamine lotion over the bite, her touch cool and soothing.

Frederick picked up his fork and ate.

Frederick woke up scratching his neck again, relieved that Julia was in the bed with him. She straddled him, her face Popsicle red. She pushed his shoulders against the mattress. Through the open window, he heard the baby crying.

"I can't help it!" she giggled. "I want one. I just want a baby so bad!"

Frederick tried to sit up, but she shoved him back down on the sand. The entire bed was drenched with seawater. He could smell the iron tanks, the metal of his gun. She laughed and grinned, revealing pointed teeth.

"You'll always be my hero, Fred." She kissed his neck and pulled him away from fear.

In the morning, Frederick stumbled downstairs in a haze. Julia served him a fried banana sandwich for breakfast. Instead of eating it, Frederick scratched at his bandaged neck.

"Don't," she said. "You'll make it worse."

He scratched again, knocking the chain of his dog tags. The metal peeled at the tape that held the gauze in place. He looked at the sandwich again, at the soft slices of yellow neatly laid atop the peanut butter, carefully fried to a golden yellow. Love. Warmth. Not cowardice, like he'd originally thought.

He removed his tags and placed them on the table. "I'll give you a child, Julia. I know that's what you want."

"Really?" she asked.

Frederick took a bite and nodded. "I'd do anything for you, darling."

She straddled him in the night.

"I love you," Frederick said. He closed his eyes and thought of red, of victory, of Julia's smile, her teeth covered with red. Then he woke to an empty room. Outside, the neighbors screamed. The mother cried. The baby didn't. The boy cried, and the father threatened to beat him if he didn't tell the truth.

"She was naked!" the boy cried. "She was here!"

Frederick hurried downstairs and found Julia on the sofa, clutching not a pillow, but the baby. She whispered in its ear, but the baby was limp, its yellow sleeper drenched in blood. Julia slurped what was left and giggled.

Frederick tried to wake her.

"Oh, Fred!" she said, smiling wider than ever. "It tastes just like I hoped it would!"

"You're sleepwalking, Julia," he said, carefully taking the infant in his steady hands. He held its lifeless weight and guided Julia into the shower, where she washed the blood away. He got her into a new nightgown and coaxed her back to sleep.

"I love you, Julia."

The little boy cried next door, trying to convince everyone he wasn't crazy.

Frederick buried the dead baby beneath the compost in the backyard. Then he made a makeshift bed on the sofa, confident that his dear wife would soon put the poor boy out of his misery.

CHAPTER 8

THE FRUITS OF WARTIME

ORIGINALLY PUBLISHED IN "RAVENS & ROSES: A WOMEN'S GOTHIC ANTHOLOGY"

The Porter estate had once been full of life, but no longer.

At night, Jacqueline walked in bare feet. She slipped from her room, toes curled over the cold hallway floor. It might have been wrong, but she delighted in digging through the places where the late Philip Porter was rumored to have hidden piles of cash. He'd been a gambler all his life, and his death left his wife, Cecelia, nearly penniless.

Whispered conversation had faded as the servants slowly left to find work elsewhere. Dust gathered. Furniture was sold. The rooms of the mansion echoed now, but the cash flowed when Jacqueline had a good night.

She ventured into the library and held a candle up to the shelves. She pulled books out, one by one, cracking the spines, shaking the bindings. The odd hundred-dollar bill slid from between the pages.

She stalked back to her room with a grin, hiding her windfall beneath the loose floorboard in her closet.

The future seemed so uncertain since the war's ending. Men returned disfigured and Cecelia often complained women were losing their proper place in society. Jacqueline didn't mind. She finally had hope. Opportunity.

She returned to her bed, reaching beneath her mattress

for the metal toffee hammer that kept her inspired in the worst of times.

———

Cecelia poked a fork into the crepe Jacqueline had made.

"Philip didn't even eat this," she said. "Why didn't he eat it, dear?"

Jacqueline swallowed and took the plate away. "Perhaps he didn't have an appetite, ma'am."

Cecelia shook her head. "Nothing feels right," she said. "Nothing is ever right anymore. I hardly see Philip, and Peter never comes by. He used to play the piano so beautifully. It always cheered me up."

Jacqueline curled her hand over Cecelia's shoulder.

Cecelia never failed to mention Peter, her firstborn son. However, she often forgot that he died in the war.

"Maybe a nap would help, ma'am? Or we could play a game of chess?"

Cecelia shook her head again, this time more vigorously. She glanced about the room, at the unpolished silver that always looked blemished and green, much like the windows. Vines crawled over what little light managed to seep through the stained glass, yet Cecelia never really saw the estate as it was. She didn't notice the pair of trousers Jacqueline had purchased the last time she went into the city.

The pants allowed for more movement, more freedom. She'd even stopped wearing her corset. Without it, she could take deeper breaths. Calmer breaths. She held her tongue less and less and pried into Cecelia's memories whenever she slipped into another spell of confusion.

"I just wish Peter would come," she said.

Jacqueline pulled out a seat. "You often speak of Philip and Peter," she said, "but what about Matthew?"

Cecelia scoffed and pounded the table. "That boy is dead to me. He's gone. He's nothing!"

"That's not true," Jacqueline said. "I've heard things. The former servants told me things, ma'am."

All Jacqueline knew of Matthew was he was the younger son who never appeared at the mansion, either in person or in photos. She'd only heard of him through rumors, none of which spoke in his favor. "Some of the servants told me that he was married," she said.

"To a Vaudeville strumpet!" Cecelia snapped. "He sent me a photo of her once, posing onstage like some common whore." She struggled to get out of her chair, and Jacqueline moved to help her. "Never speak of that man again!"

"I'm sorry, ma'am. I didn't know."

"Well, now you do," Cecelia said. "Now you're smarter and wiser, and you know best to leave things the way they are."

"Yes, ma'am," Jacqueline said.

Cecelia picked up her cane and stomped out of the dining room, tripping over the corner of the hallway carpet as she made her way to the grand stairwell.

———

Jacqueline was only ever good at making toast or sandwiches. She often tried to replicate some of Cecelia's favorite meals, only to struggle and curse herself for failing at womanly chores. She could clean well, but she was much better at meddling and sometimes, when the occasion was right, protesting.

She was slicing from an overcooked chicken breast when she heard a car pull up in the gravel driveway. She peered through the window at the black vehicle crawling into view and hesitated before throwing the entire chicken out and answering the door.

The man standing there gawked at Jacqueline's trousers. "She's got a gardener answering the door now?"

"I'm not the gardener," Jacqueline said. "I-I'm the housekeeper."

The man's gaze narrowed. "Forgive me, but you don't look at all like a housekeeper."

"I know," she said. "We've been rather short-staffed."

He pushed past her into the hall. "She wrote to me a while back," he said, surveying the dimmed gas lamps and dusty vases. "I'm sure she thought she was writing to Peter, but that alone is a sign things weren't going well."

Jacqueline shut the door and turned.

The guest had dark eyes and brown hair, his chin unshaven. The growing stubble cast a shadow over his jaw. He set his suitcase down, and Jacqueline glanced at his left hand. No ring.

"Are you Matthew?" she asked.

He nodded.

"Your mother hasn't been herself since the deaths," Jacqueline said. "She reads the paper but often forgets about the war."

He expressed no concern for Cecelia, ducking instead toward the library.

The sun slipped through the stained-glass windows, but the mahogany shelves still made the room seem darker than it actually was.

"Do you want me to call on her?" Jacqueline asked.

"Not yet," he said, picking a frame with Peter's photo off the mantle. He stared for a while before setting it down so hard, the other frames shook.

"You didn't even attend the funerals," Jacqueline said.

He turned to her, cocking a smile. "I'm sure my mother appreciated that."

"Didn't you want to pay your respects?"

"Neither of them ever paid me much respect," he said, looking at her for too long, enough to make her shift. Then he turned to the shelf she'd searched the night before.

"I don't know much about you, sir. People gossiped but—"

"You're quite forward for a servant," he said. "You're asking questions you probably shouldn't. Out of everyone, why would Mother keep you?"

Jacqueline made a fist over the shelf, straightening her spine as though she were still wearing a corset. "I was the last maid hired. In the end, I was the only one she could afford to keep."

He pushed into her personal space, gaze settling over the tapered leg of her trousers, where the fabric clung to her ankles. "So, you do *all* the cooking and cleaning?"

"I try." Jacqueline struggled to stand firm. "I try to make things seem as normal as possible. She barely has enough money to keep the gas running."

He smirked again, nodding at his suitcase in the hall. "Well, if you're a half-decent maid, I suppose I can trust you to take my things to a vacant room upstairs?"

His stare hardened her. She drew a breath, a bigger one than a corset would allow. "I can do that for you, sir."

"Matthew," he corrected. "You asked for my name. Go ahead and use it."

"Yes, sir— sorry, Matthew," she said, hurrying to retrieve his bag.

Matthew's old room faced the overgrown rear garden. Jacqueline pushed the burgundy curtains open, and the room seemed to moan beneath the light, the deep reds and mauves swelling like an open wound.

She turned back to the suitcase on the bed.

It was what servants did, was pry.

But then the piano started. The melody worked through the empty mansion like birdsong. It hypnotized Jacqueline for a moment as she fingered the latches.

Cecelia's door creaked open down the hall. She hobbled, one hand on her cane and the other skimming the paintings, tilting them askew as she rushed to follow the sound. "Peter?" she called. "Peter, is that you?"

Jacqueline left the suitcase and followed.

"Hello, Mother," Matthew said. His voice felt heavy. It echoed against the walls of the servant's corridor, where Jacqueline spied.

"Why are you here?" Cecelia snapped. "What have you come for?"

"I wanted to help," he said, getting up from the piano bench.

"What could you possibly do to help?"

"I've brought money. A bit of money." Matthew's voice slipped an octave, his tone submissive and meek. Still, he took a step toward her. Even though he stood taller, he went to her with his shoulders sloped and his head hung.

"And where is *she*?" Cecelia asked.

"She's gone, Mother."

"And I suppose this money you have was hers?"

"We settled, Mother." He fumbled with his watch chain before pressing his hands into his pockets. "It was amicable."

Cecelia sighed. "Of all the men that could return to this house, it had to be you, bringing your sin and shame with you."

"I said I wanted to help, Mother."

"What good can you do here?"

"I want to prove myself, Mother. Please, give me another chance."

She scoffed, taking a seat. "Send for the maid. Tell her I'd like some tea."

Matthew nodded slowly, then lifted his head, his pained gaze meeting Jacqueline's prying eyes. A glint slipped over his expression. Then his lip curled. Gentle. Subtle.

It made her flush.

His footsteps moved about the house, heavy and frantic as the day wore on.

Jacqueline wasn't used to the sound of a man stalking the halls, either above her or below.

He fussed about the rooms. He moved things. Rustled things.

She was now certain he'd only come for the money. She smiled to herself whenever he stole into a hiding place she'd already raided, his curses echoing off the walls.

For dinner, she prepared a filet cod. She lit a fire and positioned the candlesticks but, when it came time to bring the plates to the table, the dining room stood vacant.

Cecelia still sat in the parlor, and Jacqueline placed a hand on her shoulder, startling her from her daze.

"I've made you some dinner," she tried, but the old woman sulked over her embroidery, stabbing the needle through the cloth on her hoop.

"I refuse to eat with that boy."

"Can I at least bring you your dinner here?"

"No," Cecelia groaned. "I'm afraid I've already lost my appetite."

"There's no need to keep up appearances simply because he's here," Jacqueline said. "I'm sure he'll leave just as quickly as he came."

Cecelia shifted, her expression changing when she finally took notice of Jacqueline's trousers. "He's fond of women of ill repute, you know? The war is over. It's about time you found your place again."

Jacqueline swallowed. "Ma'am, I'm sorry, but don't imagine things will simply go back to the way they were."

"They will," she insisted. "And don't think I'll be letting you go back to those silly meetings in town when they do."

Footsteps shuffled around the servant's quarters upstairs.

Jacqueline made a fist, fighting to maintain composure.

"It's foolish," Cecelia said. "You're being foolish, thinking you'll ever have the same rights as a man."

Jacqueline swallowed, flattening her palm down the front of her apron. "Yes, ma'am."

Cecelia picked her needlework back up. She pressed the needle into the fabric with an unsteady hand, making a line of crude red Xs that looked like stitches struggling to hold reality.

Jacqueline went to clear the dining room table after putting Cecelia to bed, only to find Matthew sitting at its head, scraping the last of the fish off his plate. She gasped but caught herself when the heat from the dining room fireplace warmed her.

Matthew nodded at the other plate he'd set for her. The silver fork was tarnished, but she pulled out a chair and pressed the tines into the over-buttered filet. She bit into a long fragment of bone.

"Please tell me you haven't made her this fish before," Matthew said, snickering as she placed the bone on her plate.

Jacqueline shook her head and took another bite. She chewed, swallowed. Too much butter. Too much lemon. "I like working for your mother," she said, the slippery blend of bitter turning sour in her mouth.

"She lets you get away with far more than you ought to." He nodded at her trousers.

Jacqueline put her fork down, reaching instead for her white wine. "She trusts me."

He smirked. "She shouldn't. Nobody should trust a maid. Not now. You're all desperate."

The wine numbed as it slipped down her throat. "I'm hardly a maid, sir."

"So, she admits it, now?" he asked, picking up his own glass.

Jacqueline couldn't help but give a little. Her cheeks flushed. "I'm trying to survive."

Matthew leaned toward her, his smile now a grin. "Does that mean that I'm right to assume those are your finger-prints all over that shelf in the library?"

This time, it was Jacqueline who curled her lips, finally shedding the burden of what felt like pretend.

He had a book of sheet music from the Ziegfeld Follies 1919 show on his nightstand.

"Do you play?" she asked, fingering the crisp pages.

"Hardly," he said, snatching the book.

A photograph slipped from between the sheets, and Jacqueline bent to retrieve it. "Is this her?" she asked. "Is this your wife?"

The woman in the photo was dressed in a Follies costume, her hair cut short, and her body scantily clad with fringe and feathers.

Matthew took her wrist. He twisted her arm behind her back and shoved her face down on the bed, prying the photo from her grasp.

"Bastard!" she cried.

"Oh, she has a tongue!" Matthew said, leaning over her.

Jacqueline turned her face against the covers, struggling beneath his weight as he pulled the pins from her cap. Her hair slipped over her shoulders, and she bucked against him as he climbed over her, the sound of his aggression filling her ear.

"She likes a good ravishing, too," he growled.

"It's Jacqueline," she said.

"Jacqueline! Jacqueline with the pretty name and the luscious chestnut curls." He kissed her neck and her jaw and her cheek, slipping his hand down her side. He undid the buttons of her trousers, his hungry grasp struggling to pull the stiff cotton down her hips.

Jacqueline shuddered, her breaths deepening as she squirmed against the firming evidence of his arousal. His grunts only built as he struggled to pry her knee from her trousers.

"This is why women should wear skirts," he said. "A man shouldn't have this much trouble—"

"A man always makes trouble," she said, tugging each trouser leg off her ankles.

He undid the buttons of her shirtwaist, then tugged at the neckline of her chemise, freeing her breasts to the cold.

Her nipples hardened, and he twisted them in the pinch of his fingers, drawing a shriek from her lungs.

He buried her moan in the sheets and pried her drawers to her knees. His palm caressed her skin, softly at first. Then he bared nails. He clawed her flesh before striking her buttocks with an open palm. The sting drove her into a frenzied scramble across the bed, which only made him grasp her body like a starving predator in pursuit.

She put up a fight, but only because it was expected. Her protests only flooded her body with adrenaline, a need. She tried to twist herself from his hold, but a rush swept across her chest when he pulled her backward into the heat of his forceful embrace.

"Don't be defiant, Jacqueline. Is it so shameful? Is it so wrong to enjoy this?"

She whimpered.

His smile spread against her ear. "Everyone seems to think I'm some horrible brute, but you, Jacqueline, you suffer so beautifully for me!"

"Save your breath," she gasped. "Please, just fuck me."

"Oh, I'll talk *while* fucking you, Jacqueline," he said, bending her over, eagerly pushing his energies inside. "I'll make you know it's me taking you, that it's *me* making you writhe like a fish on a line." His palms slid against the sweat of her flesh as he thrust, and he moved his grasp over her hips, his aggression turned flustered and uneven as he increased his pace.

She clutched her fists over his sheets as she struggled to hold herself on hands and knees. Her eyes rolled back. Her vision blurred.

"Say my name!" he said.

She hesitated, and he bared his nails again.

"Matthew!" she cried, only to swoon as he groaned.

"Does it feel good, Jacqueline? Do I make you feel good?"

She nodded. She moaned. She said his name again, her breaths deepening in the friction that worked them into a tangled frenzy of release.

He covered her mouth, holding her tight until her cries of rapture spilled between his fingers.

She twisted her face to catch her breath, but he turned her over and sealed her gaping mouth with his, suffocating her with kisses until her fists beat against his chest.

He laughed and held her. "Kiss me, darling!" he said, offering his cheek.

Drunk with euphoria, she obliged.

Then he turned his other cheek. "Again."

This time, she resisted, but he gripped her curls and held her still.

"The other cheek, Jacqueline!" he growled. "Kiss me like you love me! Like you mean it!"

Her breath caught. She looked at him, searching for his smile, but it was gone, his gaze hard. Determined. Angry. She stilled her gasps and kissed his cheek, unable to hide her hesitation.

He lowered his head and withdrew.

"Matthew?" she tried.

"You can act for my mother, but not for me?"

She struggled to catch her breath, but he got off the bed. He pulled on his robe and walked to the bathroom. The faucet squeaked. He splashed his face.

Jacqueline hesitated, swallowing back the tightness in her throat. "Y-you just caught me off-guard."

The faucet squeaked again. The pipes moaned, but he didn't respond.

She glanced at the locked bedroom door, thinking of the cold that lay beyond it. The fire cracked, and she shifted her attention back to the nightstand as she pulled on her clothes. The photo of Matthew's wife was already gone. Only the book of sheet music remained.

"'*You'd Be Surprised*'," she read beneath her breath.

"That song was my favorite." Matthew stood in the bathroom doorway, his silk dressing gown hanging off his slumped shoulders.

"I hope to see a Follies show one day," she tried. "I've always wanted to live in the city, to have my own apartment."

His lips curved again. "I could play it for you tomorrow if you'd like."

She straightened her spine and raised her chin to address his approach. "I would," she said, suddenly needing to be proper, despite the heat inside of her, a fire he'd put there. "I'd love to hear you play, sir."

"*Sir*," he laughed. "That's so impersonal, Jacqueline." He sat beside her, put a hand over hers and squeezed. "Please, call me Matthew."

Jacqueline woke at dawn, splashed her face with water and confronted her reflection before digging out her maid's uniform. She pulled on the stockings and tied the garters. She hooked the corset over her frame, hating how its woven cording held her shoulders up and her head high when she knew she could do both well enough on her own when it was required. Her heels clacked down the servant's stairwell and into the kitchen, but the hob had already been used, and the kettle already boiled.

"Mother, I'd do anything to get back into your good graces!"

Jacqueline followed Matthew's voice through to the dining room. An empty plate sat at the table's head.

"Where did Eddie go?" Cecelia cried.

"I'll play again! I'll play for you, Mother! Remember how much you loved it?"

The piano came to life moments later, bleeding a soft melody through the mahogany halls.

Jacqueline's hesitant footsteps sounded on the offbeat, much like her heart had when she'd kissed Matthew the night before.

Like she loved him.

Like she meant it.

She passed through the library, where new fingerprints marked every single shelf.

Her heart pounded. The corset restricted. She pushed the parlor door open to find Matthew at the piano.

Cecelia sat slumped in her chair, struggling to poke the needle through the cloth.

"This is your favorite song, isn't it, Mother?" Matthew asked, only to change chords and tempo when he met Jacqueline's gaze.

Cecelia shook her head. "This is wrong! You're playing it wrong!"

"This is how I played it for you before, Mother," he said, passing a darkened glance at Jacqueline.

Cecelia stomped her foot. "This is that vaudeville filth!" She took her cane and tried to stand, only to stumble over the corner of the rug. She took a knee, cane skittering across the floor.

Finally, the piano stilled.

Matthew rose and lifted Cecelia. She begged for the cane, and Jacqueline rushed to retrieve it.

Cecelia swatted at her son. "I ought to call on your father!"

"Oh, there's little good he can do now," Matthew seethed.

Cecelia huffed, her eyes turning red. She leaned over the cane and slapped his face. "Get out of this house! You're no son of mine!" Tears streamed as she lifted her cane to hit him, but Matthew managed to block her strike with his arm.

"All you've ever done is hate me, Mother!"

"And for good reason!" she said, trying to swing her cane again.

Matthew staggered, but Jacqueline pulled the woman back. "Ma'am, stop. There's no need!"

Cecelia fought, but Jacqueline squeezed her shoulder, forcing the cane back into the woman's grasp before guiding her to the stairs.

"I thought he was Peter at first," Cecelia admitted. Her voice wavered as she clung to the banister.

"I understand, ma'am," Jacqueline said. "I'll admit, he is a bit of a brute."

Cecelia blinked out a tear, her foot slipping on the wooden step. Jacqueline caught her, only for the woman to moan with confusion the rest of the way to her room. "I don't feel well. It feels like waves. It feels like when the news of Peter came!"

Jacqueline tucked her into bed before pressing a cold cloth to her forehead. "Rest up, ma'am."

"Did you find a new cook? He made the most delicious crepe."

"No, ma'am, I didn't. Please rest. You'll feel better after a nap."

The piano started again, Matthew back at work, playing the song he'd promised.

"He's not so good in a crowd but when you get him alone, you'd be surprised! He isn't much at a dance but then when he's taking you home, you'd be surprised!"

"That boy's brought sin to this house again," Cecelia moaned. "I want him gone."

"He doesn't look like much of a lover, but you can't judge a book by its cover…"

His voice found the rebellious parts of her, but Jacqueline stood at Cecelia's bedside until her exhaustion gave way to sleep. Closing the door behind her, she wrung her hands in her apron, her heart beating beneath the layers of clothing that held her strict and rigid.

"He's got the face of an angel, but there's a devil in his eye!"

Matthew had closed the piano by the time she returned to the parlor.

"Where did you learn to make a proper crepe?" she asked.

He rose from the bench and buttoned his jacket. "I'm not some pompous rich boy, Jacqueline. I doubt you'd simply fuck any man who was."

She drew a breath, feeling the restriction. "You're toying

with her," she said. "You're toying with me as well, and I'd rather you didn't."

He hesitated, shifting his glance to the window and the overgrown vines. "I told her my name was Eddie, that I was a new servant. I made her breakfast. I made her tea. She was happy."

"Eddie?"

He blushed, glancing at his shoes. "After Eddie Cantor, of course."

Jacqueline kicked at the carpet where Cecelia had tripped.

"I'm not the man she makes you think I am. Surely, you must believe that, Jacqueline."

"You lied to your own mother," she said.

"She hardly considers herself my mother." He paused. "By the time she wakes, she'll remember even less of me."

Jacqueline stepped back, still tasting the fish she'd ruined.

"I do like you, Jacqueline," he said. "I like talking to you. You make all of this less painful."

She looked at him, longer than she should have. The wound in him lingered behind his smile. She tried to soften her posture, but the corset wouldn't allow it. "Why would you come back, other than your father's money?"

"I thought that if I played the piano, maybe it would trigger a memory. Maybe she would think differently of me. Maybe she'd put me back in the will. This estate must pass to someone and, if it's not Peter, it must be me."

"You can't take advantage of a lost old woman."

He gawked. "But isn't that what you're doing? She thinks just as little of you as she does of me."

"That's not true."

"She doesn't pay you," Matthew countered, "and you're not staying here out of the goodness of your heart."

She looked down at the floor.

"You're toying with her too, Jacqueline. Don't pretend."

She turned away, slipping down the servant's wing. The door swung behind her, but Matthew didn't follow.

His footsteps crept through the house all afternoon.

When Cecelia woke, she asked to play a game of chess, which Jacqueline set up in the parlor.

"The king is the weakest piece," Cecelia said, moving her white pawn. "All the other pieces move around just to protect the one that looks that strongest."

Jacqueline moved a black pawn.

"I never loved Philip," Cecelia said.

"No?" She moved her pawn again, making room for the knight to take charge.

"Oh, Jacqueline, you forget!"

"Forget what, ma'am?"

"The knight jumps, dear. It's the only piece that can jump over the others."

"Oh."

Upstairs, something clattered. Footsteps sounded, moving into the room that once belonged to Peter.

Cecelia reset the board. "Philip was at least a skilled chess player. He taught Peter well, too. I've had a great many matches with them through the years."

They started again. Cecelia moved a pawn. Jacqueline moved a different black pawn, rethinking her strategy, making room for her rook to slide.

A bang sounded above, but Cecelia failed to notice. She drew her dressing gown over her frame and shivered.

"The darkness," she said. "It's everywhere now. Can't you feel it?"

"It's because we have to keep the lights down, ma'am." Jacqueline slid her rook across the board. "Check, ma'am."

Cecelia moved a knight, only for Jacqueline to take it.

"Check again, ma'am."

Cecelia stared at the board in confusion. "You're not following the rules!"

Jacqueline hesitated. "I'm trying to fight for a better future for myself, ma'am."

"You're naive," Cecelia sneered. "The war might have

changed some things, but it won't change them all. A good man will only put up with a woman like you for so long."

Jacqueline hesitated, picking up one of her pawns, and jumping it halfway across the board. "Checkmate, ma'am."

Cecelia gawked, her memory lost again. "Well then." She shivered again and Jacqueline got up to fetch a shawl to wrap her. More rustling sounded above them. Cecelia smiled despite it. "I do love that new cook!" she said. "Eddie, wasn't it?"

"It is," she said, and Cecelia's delight spread.

"Have him make a brisket tonight," she said. "It's been so long since I've had a proper brisket."

———

Matthew cooked much better than Jacqueline. She sat atop the counter and watched him simmer and broil. He arranged a slice of brisket on a plate with potatoes and vegetables. He poured a glass of wine and placed the freshly polished silver around each plate. Jacqueline drank from the bottle, charmed by his efforts.

But when Cecelia saw Matthew, she shrieked. "Where's Eddie?" she cried. "Where's Peter?"

"Mother, please!" Matthew begged. "I'm here! I'm trying to help!"

She struck his shoulder with her cane.

Matthew staggered, but Cecelia swung again, barely missing the cheek that Jacqueline had forced herself to kiss.

———

Jacqueline calmed Cecelia in the aftermath. She bathed her, dressed her, pulled the covers over her.

"What did I do to end up with him?" Cecelia asked. "Why did the wrong son die?" Her cries worked through the halls like a trumpet before the war.

There was nothing Jacqueline could do to console her, so she left the room and found Matthew in the main hall, sitting before the fire, a drink in his hand. Cecelia's cane cracked in the flames.

Her lips parted to confront him, but Matthew rubbed at his shoulder. She took the empty seat before the fire instead. "Why does she hate you so much?"

"Because I'm just a shadow," he said, taking a sip of his brandy. "I could never be better than Peter, so I sought different influences, none of which she approved of." He lifted the bottle and poured more liquor into a second glass. "I've worked," he said. "I've bled and I've struggled, Jacqueline. I know what it's like to have no other choice."

He pushed the glass toward her. She took it, and he smiled. He rubbed his shoulder again.

"Is it bad?" she asked.

"It's nothing a drink can't fix. Nothing you can't fix." He rose with his drink and knelt before her chair. Jacqueline pressed a hand beneath his jacket. She curved her palm over the bruise and pressed. He winced, then eased his hand up her skirts.

"You're a proper maid today," he said, reaching between her thighs, up her drawers, into her folds.

She hammered his bruised shoulder, but he only prodded deeper, his fingers curling, finding the spongy bit inside of her that made her melt into his hold.

"Don't pretend you don't like it," he said, rising. He set his drink down and cupped her chin with his free hand. He forced her to look at him, pinching at her lips, manipulating the sounds that came from her mouth much like he did the keys of the piano. His pressure burned at her, and she writhed and moaned until he pulled his hand from beneath her skirts. He pushed his fingers past her lips and forced her to taste herself. "You don't have to pretend with me, Jacqueline."

"I know," she said, shaking her head, which felt wrong, considering she was agreeing with him.

Matthew laughed, hooking his fingers against her cheek. "My little fish," he said, drawing her up and into his arms.

The fireplace raged in his bedroom. Afterwards, she kissed him on one cheek and then the other, her insides burning from the shame of what she assumed would be ritual.

"Tell me you love me," he said. "Like you mean it."

Her brows furrowed, unable to hide her reaction.

"Say it! Say it now!" He shook her, rattled her.

"No. I can't. I'm not an actress! I'm just a stupid maid!"

Her words dismantled him. He pulled away and groaned, doubling over on the side of the bed, face cupped in his hands. He breathed heavily, frantic.

Jacqueline scrambled off the bed, reaching for her clothes.

"Please don't go," he begged. "I know I can be a bit much at times."

Her better instincts told her to leave, but then she'd be alone again. Misunderstood again. Her chest burned, but she savored the heat of it, the malice of it.

Matthew drew closer. "If you want the truth, I'll tell you. I know how to cook because I worked at a restaurant in New York when I first left home." He touched her back, his hand wet.

She wasn't sure if it was with her own lust or his tears.

"I'm really not so hopeless," he said.

She glanced at the nightstand, noticing the flimsy dog-eared book that sat where the sheet music had.

The Way of a Man with a Maid. The author was anonymous.

She reached for the book, and he didn't stop her.

"My wife wasn't so happy when she discovered that printing in the back of my dresser."

Her fingers shifted over the worn pages. Some of them were stained with fingerprints, the corners folded over to mark specific passages of the narrator ravaging a helpless woman. A photo tucked into the book's sixth chapter put her face to face with his former wife. It was a different picture from the night before; this time, her eyes were blacked out with ink.

"One would think that for an actress, she would have been more willing to entertain my proclivities. Instead, she treated me just as Mother does."

Her eyes skimmed the page, depicting a scene where the narrator forced his captive to give him a kiss. Jacqueline pressed the photo back into the book's spine. She closed her eyes and willed her heart to stop throbbing.

"My wife thought it was in her best interest to rid herself of me," he said, voice cracking. "I had nowhere else to go. I had to come, and here you are!" He touched her shoulder and kissed the tender flesh of her neck. His stubble scratched it. Then, firming his grasp, he bared teeth.

Jacqueline shrieked, but Matthew clung to her as though she were an object, a possession, a comfort toy poised to give a child a blissful night of sleep.

"You act every day, Jacqueline," he fawned, licking her, tasting her. "You're good at it, except with me!"

"I had no choice," she said. "I have no skills, and I might soon have nothing."

He pulled her back into his embrace, her legs wrapped around his waist.

She thought to fight but didn't. Couldn't. She let him enter her again and he worked her up and down, reshaped her with his sweaty palms.

He clung so tightly that his hands shook, and his breath vibrated. "You could have me, Jacqueline, if you wanted me."

She stiffened. "Wanted you?"

"I'd take good care of you," he promised. "I'd give you whatever you asked for."

"I'm not an actress," she said again.

"You already play a passing maid. Playing a wife would be second nature."

Her throat tightened. "I can't."

"You *can*."

She climbed off, but he remained on the bed, naked, all his desire exposed.

"Please, Jacqueline," he begged. "You know me. You've felt me. Don't think ill of me."

She put on her clothes and backed against the door. "Truthfully, you scare me a little."

He rolled his bruised shoulder and shifted. His gaze darkened. "It's much scarier out there, Jacqueline."

"I've been out there before."

"Oh, have you?"

She felt for the knob, the cold of the metal stealing heat from her palm. "I—I honestly don't plan on staying here that long. I want to live in the city. I want to take care of myself."

He set the book back on the nightstand. "I'm a good man," he said, positioning it just as it had been before she'd picked it up. "I'm a careful man. Most wouldn't think so, but I hoped you would. I thought you did."

The fire cracked, and she twisted the knob, the floor like ice beneath her feet. She waited in the dark for him to protest but only heard him putting a new log on the fire.

In the morning, Jacqueline woke up and splashed water on her face. "He's just a man," she said to the mirror. "He's a stupid brute of a man. Don't let him get the best of you."

His music rang through the house, and Jacqueline took Cecelia to the gardens to escape.

Without her cane, she stumbled, and Jacqueline threaded her arm through hers. "Eddie plays such delightful music," Cecelia said. "And he has a watch that looks just like Peter's."

Jacqueline clung to the old woman's arm. "There is no Eddie," she said. "There is no Peter, either. I'm afraid there's only me, ma'am."

"Oh, nonsense," Cecelia laughed. "You've been so distracted, Jacqueline, with all your meetings."

Jacqueline hesitated, her foot skidding over a loose pebble. "I haven't gone to a meeting in months, ma'am."

"It's all for the best," she said. "The city streets are no place for a proper woman."

"What if I don't want to be a proper woman?" Jacqueline asked, but Cecelia slipped out of her hold. The overgrown brush slapped her cheeks and caught her hair. Crows squawked above, leaving Jacqueline no choice but to take the old woman back inside, where Matthew's song lulled Cecelia back into her chair.

When it came time to pay the bills, Jacqueline found the bank account entirely dry. She dimmed the gas and struggled to warm Cecelia's hands and feet before the parlor fireplace. Cecelia's numb fingers barely managed to poke through the fabric of her embroidery, and the roses she attempted to stitch grew distorted. Its petals looked swollen. Its thorns curled.

Matthew cooked lamb and vegetables, and the three ate dinner over candlelight.

"I hate when the darkness of fall creeps in," Cecelia observed, struggling to cut through her meat.

"Would you like some help, ma'am?" Jacqueline asked.

"I've got it," Matthew said, pulling his chair closer. "Here you are, Mother." He sliced her meat, then lifted the fork to her lips.

"I can do it myself, Eddie."

"Peter," he said. "Don't you remember, Mother? I'm not Eddie. I'm Peter, your son."

"No, you're not Peter." She took Matthew's face in her hands, but her confusion gave way when Matthew pushed another forkful of lamb past her lips.

Jacqueline reached for her wine.

"You know what I miss?" Matthew asked. "A good corset. I appreciate the way a corset can make a woman sit up straight and proper."

"Yes, Peter!" Cecelia said, chewing through the tender

meat. "You're so right! These women now, they have no dignity left."

Jacqueline found her spine in response.

"Just like that," Matthew said, pointing.

Beside him, Cecelia laughed. "Oh, Jacqueline, you have become quite foolish with all your meetings and such!"

"Meetings?" Matthew asked.

"She used to ask for evenings off, twice a week," Cecelia said, struggling to chew.

Matthew held her wine to her lips, giving her a sip.

Cecelia smiled, patting Matthew's hand in gratitude. "She kept saying it was to visit family, but I figured it out. You would have laughed if you were here when I confronted her, Peter! She still thinks it's worth all this time and effort just for a silly vote!"

Matthew's face crumpled. He drew a breath to speak, but Jacqueline lifted her glass, easing her tension with inebriation.

———

After putting Cecelia to sleep, Jacqueline passed through the empty halls and into the narrow corridors of the servant's wing. No footsteps. No hunt. She set the candle on the nightstand, only for its light to touch Matthew's shadow emerging from behind the door.

"You startled me!" she said.

The candlelight flickered as he took her. He undressed her desperately, tearing at the laces of her corset, shedding her layers like skin to the icy floor.

The springs of her narrow bed squeaked beneath her back as he toyed with her. He pleased her with his hands, then finished himself inside her.

She drew in full breaths, but rapture only lasted so long when he leaned in for his kiss. She pushed him away.

"The maid kisses him in the book," Matthew insisted.

"I don't care."

"But you've already kissed me! You kissed me passionately."

"I didn't kiss you with passion," she confessed.

Matthew straightened. "What was it, then?"

"Pity."

His expression hardened. He climbed off her, head hung. A cold wind rattled against the window.

Jacqueline drew a breath.

"You know what happens to girls like you in the city? All those flappers at the speakeasy are just desperate sluts with nowhere to go."

She seized beneath his glare.

"And you want to be one of them?" he asked. "You really aim to be one of them? Mother knows you're one of them and she lets you stay here!" He moved to her dresser.

"Don't!" she cried, but he dug into the back of the bottom drawer and immediately found her suffragette sash and hat, decorated with striped white and gold ribbon.

He raged. "Why would Mother even let you leave the house in these?"

"Because she respects me," Jacqueline spat.

"Respects you?" he asked, fists shaking over the ribbon. "She laughed at you!"

He draped the sash over her frame, set the hat on her head, and pinned it into place over her tangled locks. "If I could just have a picture of you! If I could show it to her, show her what you really are. Just a filthy suffragette who steals and lies and forces her husband to do all her work!"

Jacqueline went to take off the hat, but he shoved her back.

"I'm fighting for myself!" she cried. "When I leave this house, I'll have nothing! I have no rights!"

"And getting a vote is going to change that?" He clutched at the sash, bringing it round her neck so the stripes coiled and cut her breaths.

Her heart raced, and she beat her fists against his chest.

Matthew clutched her wrists. He climbed over her, pinning her against the mattress. "I bet you have a hammer, don't you, just like those women in London?"

"No!" she cried. She turned away from him, glancing up at the headboard, giving her secrets away.

He reached over her head and beneath the mattress, finding the little toffee hammer that she often clutched at night, hoping its cold touch would help her one day shatter her own glass.

"She doth protest!" he laughed, shaking the hammer before her face.

"I'd never use it! I've only ever marched, Matthew, I swear!"

"Then why have it?" he demanded, grasping at the sash's hold on her neck.

She coughed and sputtered, blinking back tears. "Because it—it inspires me. It gives me hope—"

He yanked the ribbon. "I was wrong about you, wasn't I? You want nothing to do with me! You don't want to marry me, or give me children, or bless me with the love I deserve!"

"I'm scared," she choked. "You're scaring me, Matthew."

"Then kiss me!" he cried. "Tell me you want me! Tell me you love me!"

So, she did, with the sour stench of brandy and tears between them. One cheek. Then the other. Then on the lips, his sobs filling her throat, tugging at her empathy, his grasp slipping from the ribbons. She drew a breath and clung before he could fully slip away.

"I want you. I love you." Her lungs ached as his tears spilled. She rubbed his bruised shoulder until his whimpering ceased. Then he laid his head between her breasts, and she held him until the metal hammer was warm between their bodies and their frenzied breaths were even. Synchronized.

"I promise I'll take care of you," he said. "I'll give you all the things a proper woman deserves."

She glanced at the pile of clothes on the floor, dreading the morning when she'd have to put them all back on.

"You don't have to wear a costume," he said. "You don't belong in this room."

She shook her head again. She agreed with him again. "I do love you, Matthew," she said, swallowing back the sour taste of the words.

He clutched her like a possession, then slowly brought himself to sit up. He lifted the hammer and threw it at the window, shattering the glass to let in the winter cold.

———

"He's just a man," she said, staring at herself in his bathroom mirror. She dressed in costume and walked downstairs into the library, where Cecelia sat at the desk with a newly-drafted will.

"No, Mother. Peter doesn't start with a P. It starts with an M."

"Don't be silly!" she insisted, trying to write her favored son's name. "It can't start with an M."

"I'd never steer you wrong, Mother," he said. "It can, and it does. Now just write the points." He directed her to spell the rest, then lifted his gaze, meeting Jacqueline's prying eyes. A glint slipped over his expression, and his lip curled. Intent. Sinister.

It would have made her body go cold if she wasn't so cold already.

———

On the day of the first snow, Matthew went to the bank to pay the bills.

Cecelia watched him drive off through the parlor window. "What a good man he is, that son of mine!"

"That's not Peter, ma'am," Jacqueline said. "That's Matthew, and he is truly vile."

Cecelia laughed, stabbing the needle into her hoop, her rose now a massive span of red that bled in all directions. "Matthew died, dear. He's always been dead to me."

Jacqueline wanted to scream, but she couldn't, not when she was wearing a corset and the proper amount of petticoats to protect her from the house's chill. She struggled to kneel, adding another log to the fire. Even her hands were cold now, but she warmed them in her skirts and squeezed her way up the drafty servant's stairwell to her former room. She dug into the floorboards, only to find that Matthew had taken all the money she'd stored away.

She cried until her insides burned with fury.

The door squeaked open, and Matthew's gasp fogged in the cold. "Come here, Jacqueline," he said, lifting her off the floor and into his embrace. He carried her over the threshold of his room, where the fire raged. He buried her in his covers, then tossed her suffragette ribbons over the flames.

"You took my money," she said.

He knelt over the bed and smiled. "It's in an account. It's part of the estate now."

"You took everything!" she cried.

"I'm *giving* you everything!" He reached into his jacket, and pulled out a tiny, hinged box.

She shook her head, but he grabbed her left hand. She fought and twisted, but he persisted, wrestling the icy metal of Cecelia's diamond ring over her knuckle.

"Say it!" he said. "Make me the happiest man in the world, Jacqueline! Do it, now!"

"It was my money!" she screamed. "It was mine!" She always thought herself a formidable foe against Cecelia, always several moves ahead, but Matthew grabbed her face and wrestled her lips to form words.

He twisted the ring, bending her fingers until the flimsy bones threatened to break. "You'll never have to leave, Jacqueline! You won't even need to care for Mother! I'll even show you how to get all the bones out of a fish!"

Check.

Checkmate.

She withered in his arms, held so tight and dear that the storm of kisses he showered over her left her weak and empty, with no choice but to accept everything he offered.

———

She splashed her face in the morning and tried to pry the ring off her finger. "He's just a man," she said, but the ring was too tight, and it clung to her swollen knuckle.

She left Matthew's room for the grand staircase stairwell, thinking back to her first day at the Porter Estate, when she'd looked up those mahogany steps and imagined herself descending just like a proper woman would. Now, she gripped the banister. She closed her eyes, and lifted her skirts to take the first step, only to scream.

Cecelia lay at the bottom, mouth contorted, her body stiff and her gaze frozen, staring at Jacqueline with an expression of permanent confrontation.

Around her lay the scattered pages of the book of sheet music she'd slipped on.

You'd Be Surprised.

———

Matthew's music rang through the house at Cecelia's funeral.

He'd invited friends from New York and herded them all into the parlor.

Jacqueline took her time getting ready, struggling to pin her hair back just like the women in the fashion magazines. She didn't want a lady's maid. She didn't need someone prying. Someone judging. She pinned a black hat into place and made her way to the stairs.

Downstairs, Matthew switched tempo and tone. Classical to Vaudeville.

Jacqueline clung to the banister, desperate not to slip as he sang.

"I may look simple but I want you to know, I've been to college.

I'm full of knowledge! I'm right at home with brainy men and them my wisdom I show, but when there's clever girls around, I get up and go! Oh, those educated babies are a bore. I'm gonna say what I've said many times before."

The crowd laughed in the parlor, and they kept laughing when Jacqueline entered. Matthew glanced over. He continued to play, to sing, beckoning her forward with a tilt of his head.

"Oh, the dumber they come, the better I like 'em, 'cause the dumb ones know how to make love!"

His fingers worked over the keys to the crowd's delight. Then he turned on the bench and pulled Jacqueline over his lap.

The crowd of strangers whistled and hollered and cheered.

"Everyone, I'd like to introduce you to my wife, Jacqueline!" he announced.

The crowd crooned and chuckled as Jacqueline did what was custom, kissing him on one cheek. Then the other.

CHAPTER 9
WOMAN OF THE WHITE COTTAGE

1912

ORIGINALLY PUBLISHED IN "ANOMALIES & CURIOSITIES: AN ANTHOLOGY OF GOTHIC MEDICAL HORROR"

The man made good work of the tree. His ax slipped into the trunk, severing limbs and revealing the wood's rotted insides. He exerted so much effort while making his task seem easy.

Mary found herself fixated. She stood at her door, flesh prickling hot with the rash that kept her isolated in her cottage, often for days on end. Normally the rash affected her hands, but now the burn shifted to her chest, making her heart beat sparks inside her. With that prickling came a desire. A need.

She made the man a cup of black tea and pushed at her screen door. Her hesitant steps sunk into the mud as she crossed her strawberry patch to meet him.

"Thank you," he said, lifting the cup to his lips. "You're very kind."

His smile closed the vastness of the sky. It made the woods feel a little less expansive. The tea flushed his cheeks and warmed his strong demeanor. He handed her the empty cup, taking notice of the red bumps on her hands.

"It's only a rash," Mary said.

"But what might be the cause?"

Mary took a step back and stumbled, getting dirt on her skirt. "I've always had it. It comes and goes."

"Can I see?" he asked, reaching out.

Mary hesitated, feeling the prickle in her stomach as she offered herself to him. He ran his fingers over her skin, his grit scratching the itch, if just for a moment.

"It doesn't look very pleasant," he said. "It looks quite aggravating, if I'm honest."

"Sometimes it drives me mad," she said, pulling away.

The man returned to the tree.

Mary watched him from her doorstep, clinging to its frame as his shoulders stretched the fabric of his linen shirt. He chopped the limbs off the lifeless trunk. He twisted the shorted branches off with bare hands. Then he carried the log away, his steps leaden down the long and narrow path that led into town.

Once he was gone, Mary pressed her lips to the mug where he had drunk. She could taste him in the bergamot.

Mary didn't go into town often.

She avoided it if she could. She hated the open sky and the voices echoing around her. The residents made a spectacle of her for being childless and alone. Not to mention the rash, its shameful red reappearing whenever she found herself strained.

A part of her wanted to leave the cottage to find the man, but her better instincts told her to remain enclosed in her white cottage, protected for as long as her food and water lasted.

She kept the cottage clean. She always swept, always washed, always brought flowers in to dry. She hung them upside down in her windows, their delicate petals preventing curious townspeople from looking in.

The second time the man came, Mary stood in her garden, turning grapefruit rinds over her strawberry patch to trap the slugs.

"Do you have any more?" he asked. "I do love a ripe grapefruit."

Mary looked back to her cottage door, her mouth dry. She wound her fists over her sleeves, trying to hide the growing rash.

The man reached into his coat pocket. "This might help your hands," he said, holding out a bottle of salve.

Despite the burn, she allowed the spring sunlight to grace her skin.

"Nathaniel Edwards," he said. "I recently moved into town."

"Oh," she said, wondering if that was the reason why he'd taken the log—to build his own cabin. It was a romantic thought, a silly one. Even she knew that. Nobody would build a cabin with an infected log. "My name is Mary."

His smile widened. "Some of the people in town have spoken of you."

"Hopefully not all bad things."

Nathaniel cocked his head and took a step closer, glancing down at the grapefruit rind in her hand. "They joke of you being a witch, but we all know witches are purely fiction. Is that not the truth, Mary?"

His sly smile spread the warmth from her hands. The prickle worked up her chest and into her face, her cheeks, her lips. His kindness turned her caution into a smile, which she found herself unable to hide.

The third time, Nathaniel came to her in the night. A rock tapped against the window, and Mary climbed out of bed to find him standing before the cottage with a bundle of hand-picked wildflowers. Mary clutched at the curtains. Dried flower petals slipped to the floor.

She was hesitant to tell him that the salve he'd given her only made the rash worse. The itch spread across her chest and down her belly. It traveled down and festered into an itch in her loins.

Nathaniel approached the door, his mud-soaked boots weighing over the doorstep. She liked his throat up close. She liked seeing his nerves in his swallow.

His Adam's Apple seemed to bob in the most neglected part of her.

She pulled the door open and let him in.

Jezebel.

He left dirt in her bed. Dirt on the sheets and on the floorboards, a trail of footprints leading out the door and back down the long narrow path to town. Mary watched him disappear, the emptiness of the forest creeping closer, reaching in through the windows to touch her.

She shut the door and locked it. Then she cleaned the dirt off her floor, frantic, her limbs shaking. She scrubbed and polished and rinsed Nathaniel's scent out of her sheets, still hearing his husky whisper calling her Jezebel at the peak of lust.

After putting on a clean linen dress, she found a vase for the flowers he'd given her. She arranged them nicely on the dining table, blinking at the white blossoms until sleep took her, took the rash away, made everything normal again.

Nathaniel didn't show up again for a while.

For days.

Mary sat restlessly before the window, craving the comfort of release. She scratched at the rash through her dress until she dared to step beyond her property and toward the river where she had first seen him. The riverbank sucked at the heels of her boots, threatening to pull her into the earth. She dipped her iron kettle into the cool water but slipped in the dew and got her white dress dirty, her hands dirty. She wiped at her face and got mud on her cheek.

Somebody coughed behind her, forcing her to turn.

"There you are, dear Jezebel."

She swooned, her body giving, pleading, screaming until

the grit of his hands scratched all of her itches away. She cried tears of relief, but Nathaniel only left more dirt behind.

The rash returned.

Mary scrubbed and swept and gasped until her chest tightened. She shook the sand out of her sheets and climbed back into bed, still feeling the grains of earth between her toes. She fell asleep staring at the severed flowers on the kitchen table, their petals still lively and reaching for the light.

Mary went into town on Saturday.

The people were in the streets, moving from shop to shop, passing glances. Mary kept her chin down but her will strong. In the general store, she bought ingredients to make a lemon cake: flour and sugar and baking soda, and a little bottle of vanilla extract. She pulled the cork and savored its strength. Lost in the moment, she licked at the top of the bottle, tasting him. She tilted the bottle and took a drink. The black fluid slipped down her throat, bitter, strong, and numbing.

The shopkeeper gasped.

"I'm sorry," Mary said. "I was daydreaming."

The bell above the door rang, and she looked over to see Nathaniel. Her heart fluttered, and she found herself smiling, teeth showing. Too blunt, too eager.

He didn't mirror her delight. His lips parted, but he averted his gaze, turning to the canned goods.

Mary's breath caught.

The shopkeeper cleared his throat, drawing Nathaniel's attention. "A quick word, Doctor?"

Looks passed between shop patrons as Nathaniel's footsteps worked across the wood floors.

Whispers started, saying her name.

Mary, oh, Mary.

Mary stumbled, unable to pull her sleeves over the growing rash. The bottle of vanilla slipped from her fingers.

It rattled over the wood floor as the dark liquid sputtered from the opening, an open wound.

The whispers built. They sounded like rain against windows, and Mary's limbs stiffened as she turned for the door. A young female patron stepped in front of it.

"You see, Doctor!" she said, pointing. "The red is on her neck now!"

Nathaniel. His name.

Doctor. His title.

"H-he, he cleared a tree by the river," Mary stuttered. "He brought me medicine, though it only seemed to make things worse—"

Nathaniel shook his head. "I'm afraid you have me confused with someone else, miss." He forced a widened smile and extended a hand. "Mary, was it?"

Mary's chest flushed, and she pulled at the collar of her dress, trying to scratch the itch. She dropped the flour, the salt, the baking soda. A mountain of white piled at her feet. "I-I thought y-you wanted to help me."

Nathaniel's gaze darkened, focusing on Mary and the spectacle she was. Whispers turned to spoken words. Judgement. Laughter sounded. She felt the voices crawling beneath her skin.

"Mary, the townspeople are very concerned—"

"He-he's lying!" she insisted. "He knocked on my door, and he came inside."

Jezebel.

Nathaniel shook his head, stepping closer. "Please, Mary, don't embarrass me with your wild fantasies."

"He fancied me!" she shrieked. "I'm sure of it!"

Behind him, mouths opened into blackness. Gasps vibrated against her ears like gusts of wind.

Strumpet. Harlot. Hysterical.

Mary stepped back, shoes slipping in the spilled flour. She left footprints, trails of white winding through the shocked store patrons as Nathaniel tried to reach her before she fainted.

She gasped, her breaths shallow and paced. Her skin prickled. Her heart raced.

White walls.

White ceiling.

Sunlight glared through glass, but the window above the bed she woke in wasn't hers.

Mattress wires poked her back. She rolled her head from the brightness to the shadow of a man. This time, he was the one in white.

A white shirt. A white coat. A bottle of white smelling salts, which he moved away from her face.

"Good morning, Mary," Nathaniel said.

Mary glanced around the room, from white wall to white wall, bordered with white wainscoting and white molding, clinical—unlike her cottage, which she'd accented with lace and dried flora. This room had a dresser. There was a chair and a light.

A nurse stood in the open doorway.

"Where am I?" She tried to sit up, but restraints caught her wrists and ankles. She twisted against them, but they were tethered to the edges of the bed. She looked at Nathaniel. "You did this? You brought me here?"

"I work here, Mary," he said. "I'm the new doctor, Dr. Edwards. It would greatly benefit you if you referred to me as such."

She shook her head, trying to find the truth in his eyes. His gaze only hardened over her shaking figure, buried beneath the starched fabric of a hospital gown.

"You lied to me," she said.

"I didn't lie to you."

"Let me go!" She turned to the nurse, throat tightening as she struggled. "I don't belong here! He tricked me! He came to me! He laid with me!"

Dr. Edwards leaned closer and touched the burning rash on her bound wrist. "I promise you are safe, Jezebel. I'm going to make you better, if you'll let me in."

Mary opened her mouth, and her gasp echoed in the near-empty room—but then the nurse came with a needle.

Dr. Edwards took it.

"No, please!"

"You need rest, Mary." He grabbed her arm, and the puncture felt like nothing, like calm.

The drugs slipped into the resistance inside her.

It was so easy to fall asleep.

———

The nurse roused her in the morning.

"Dr. Edwards insisted that you have a private room," she said, undoing Mary's bindings. "He has high hopes for your treatment here, and so do I."

The nurse smiled too wide, as though trying to make a friend. "We all hope to learn a lot about treating women like you."

Jezebel.

"I'm not a bad person," Mary insisted.

The nurse sighed and glanced at the rashes climbing up her arms. "You've been a subject of gossip for quite some time, Mary. I think it's about time to make a change."

Mary shook her head, not wanting to imagine a life beyond her cottage and its familiarity. Yet she was there, in an asylum now, in a different white room that felt too clean and too sanitized. It smelt of bleach and ammonia. The sheets burned her skin when she rolled out of bed.

"Let us get you some breakfast, Mary."

The nurse led her though the maze of corridors to the cafeteria. She pulled out a chair among the other women who were supposed to be hysterical like her. None of them looked or acted like Mary. One of the women cradled a doll. "I call her Mary," she said as she pretended to nurse the doll. Then she turned and smashed its face on the table.

Another woman laughed.

Another cried.

"You're quite alright, Mary," the nurse said. "Just listen and obey, and soon you'll be home again."

Mary took her spoon and tried to eat her porridge without shaking. Sunlight glared through the big windows, pocking her chest with rashes that burned with shame.

She wanted to tell the nurse that she wasn't like these women. She was just lonely. Desperate. Scared.

She thought Nathaniel was trying to help her.

She thought he meant well.

Her gaze wandered the tiled room, but ultimately settled upon the floor. It was marked with glistening trails that wove between the tables and through the doorways.

The nurse walked away but didn't leave a trail, and Mary dropped her spoon, suddenly sick, suddenly needing to scratch. She rose and followed the clearest line of slime.

It led her down a long corridor, down a set of stairs, and into another hallway full of windows. Heat beamed in. She squinted and shielded her eyes before opening a door that led into the auditorium.

Her breath echoed in the vast space.

Paranoid. Afraid.

The beams of the ceiling rose over her like the open sky, but she kept her head low. She hurried across the empty span of the floor and found another door, which led to another hallway full of open offices that glared like eyes.

She heard his voice speaking to another. "I firmly believe that I've found a most suitable candidate for my studies. She exhibits hysterical symptoms, both the mental and physical. I believe I could even write a paper on her treatment."

Mary scratched at the heat, her moan echoing.

Then, a shadow.

Nathaniel appeared in one of the doorways, lips parting when he spotted her.

"Jezebel. What are you doing here?"

Her heart raced. She turned and ran, only to hear his footsteps hammering the tiled floor, a white coat in pursuit.

She ventured back the way she thought she'd come, pushing through the door and into a different hallway. Behind the next door waited another office wing. Behind the next, a patient wing.

"Mary!" he called.

She hurried, chest burning at the sound of her name. She twisted another knob and found a stairwell.

Mary stood at the top, fists gripping the wrought iron railing as the sunlight burned her back. She leaned over the railing and stared at the floors below, imagining herself getting to the bottom faster than anyone could chase her. She imagined her body hitting the floor, broken and torn, weathering into ash atop the marble tiles.

Such an unnatural place for one to die.

The door opened behind her. It wasn't Nathaniel, but the nurse. "Mary, dear, you have to return to your room. You can't be running about the facility like this. You'll get yourself lost."

"I'm not lost," Mary said.

The nurse took her elbow, but she wrestled herself away and continued down the stairwell, the railing scratching beneath her palm. She glanced up at the following nurse, only to crash into another body.

She smelt bergamot and gasped.

"You sure look lost to me, Mary," Nathaniel said. His gaze overwhelmed her, just like the trees in the forest. She stumbled, only to look back at the nurse, whose smile had faded and given way to judgment.

"I'm *not* lost!" she said again. "There is *nothing* wrong with me!"

"Oh, Mary," the nurse said, her gaze lingering upon her ripe red flesh.

Nathaniel grasped her shoulder. "Get her a jacket," he said.

"You're a fallen woman," he said.

The orderlies laughed and twisted the white sleeves around her frame.

"You hurt yourself. You've shamed yourself with your hysterics."

Mary shook her head. "I did nothing!" she gasped. Behind her, the orderlies tied the straitjacket like corset knots.

Nathaniel leaned over her shoulder, breath against her ear. "But you must have done *something*, Jezebel. Your shame is festering."

The orderlies chuckled, unfazed. They snickered instead of believing.

Jezebel.

"Please!" She looked to the orderlies, her sobs pleading as they completed the task of restricting her. "He's lying! He is *lying*!"

"They are only here to help you. Everyone is trying to help."

The nurse entered and placed a new stainless-steel tray on the table. On it was a new needle, drawn full of relief. Mary twisted in her binds.

"Beg for it," Nathaniel said.

The sight of it flushed her, made her itchy, made her writhe. Everyone could see it, even through the white of the straitjacket.

Jezebel. Jezebel. Jezebel.

"I want to go home," she cried.

"You can't control yourself at home," Nathaniel said.

The nurse glanced at Mary's tear-stained face and swallowed.

"You knocked," Mary said, her face burning. "You knocked on my door and you made it worse."

His lip twitched. "Would you like a *different* door, Mary? A padded cell, perhaps?"

"You brought me flowers! You left your dirt in my bed!"

The orderlies hollered.

"Stop—"

"Beg, Mary!" he yelled, reaching for the needle. "Beg for sleep! Beg for relief!"

Mary screamed as the nurse left. The orderlies forced her back onto the bed, wrestling her ankles into the bindings, ratcheting a strap over the itchiest part of her chest. Sand scraped into her flesh, grains embedding, settling, pressing hard, making it so hard to breathe.

"Please!"

The needle slipped into her skin, and the drug filled her veins until she felt like earth was burying her.

Porridge. Its blandness tasted like dirt on Mary's tongue.

Beside her, the woman with the doll lifted spoonfuls to its stitched smile. "Take it, Mary," she said.

Mary traced the glistening trails across the cafeteria with her eyes. They were fresh, morning trails of slime leading to the group of orderlies snickering in the corner.

Slugs, she thought.

Whenever she ran out of grapefruit rinds, she had to re-sort to using salt to keep the slugs from her strawberries. She hated killing, but she couldn't help but watch as their bodies twisted and contorted against the grains.

A nurse approached and touched her shoulder.

"It's time for your examination, Mary," she said. She led her by the arm, down the maze of hallways and doors and stairwells, into a room containing a wall of cabinets and a metal table with stirrups.

From one of the cabinets, the nurse pulled out a stainless tray of sanitized metal instruments.

Mary swallowed. "There is nothing wrong with me."

Instead of reassuring her, the nurse frowned. "Your rash has gotten worse since you were admitted. Dr. Edwards needs to figure out what is causing it, and he cannot do that without examining you." She set down the tray and motioned for Mary to climb on top of the stirrup table. The cold metal creaked beneath her weight.

Then the door opened, and Nathaniel entered, again in his white coat, pen in his pocket, stethoscope around his neck.

"Mary," he said with a smile, glancing over at the table before dismissing the nurse.

Mary wanted to shake her head but thought of the straitjacket, of the restraints, and the orderlies.

The nurse glanced back while leaving, lips pursed.

Nathaniel approached Mary with no words and slipped his hand beneath the neckline of her gown, exposing her chest to the clinic's sanitized air. "My, how flushed you are," he said, pressing the end of the stethoscope to her chest.

She gripped the edge of the table as her paranoia beat into his ears.

She moaned a little.

He smiled a little.

"Take a deep breath," he said, gripping her shoulder, ruining what careful intimacy she could remember with his cold commands.

The rash burned up her neck and onto her cheeks. She shut her eyes, allowing the tears to break.

Nathaniel turned to the tray of instruments. "Easy, Mary," he said, easing a tongue depressor past her lips, forcing her to open her mouth.

He forced new intimacy—shining a light into her eyes, a scope into her ears. He pressed his fingers against her neck and her stomach, her wrists and her groin, leaning in so close, so tense, his attention focused solely on how her body betrayed her.

He pushed on her chest to ease her onto her back, but she resisted.

"Lay down, Mary," he commanded, reaching for the speculum.

She shook her head and met his eyes, ones that had stared down at her in the night as he made her feel like a different woman, a relieved woman. In the sterile room, his hardened gaze proved he would never again be the man who had entered her cottage.

"I want to go home," she pleaded.

"Not until I say so, Mary." He gripped her thigh and pulled her leg into the stirrup.

The metal shook, rattling in the room's empty space. Mary braced herself on the table's edge.

"You know what will happen if you refuse to comply," he said. "The orderlies already know how to tame you. Do I need their help, or can you be good for me?"

Jezebel.

She stared at the ceiling, drawing a shaky breath as she lifted her other leg into the second stirrup. For him, she parted her knees. For herself, she let him back inside of her body with sterile steel that widened and revealed. He probed and shone a light and wrote her chart, all while she held her breath and tried not to cry as the burn worked inside of her.

When he was done, he sighed and pulled the speculum out, placing it on the tray of sullied metal. Its slick blades glistened in the light.

It was the nurses who lingered now, who glanced and grimaced when they saw her.

Jezebel.

Mary ate her porridge and tried to think back to her white cottage, the isolation of it, the notoriety of it. Did she really have other men there, like the nurses said? Did she lure them there with tea and fruit and freshly baked cakes?

Have other hands mauled her, ruined her?

Was she nothing but dirt?

The nurses' laughter drove her from her seat and the dining hall. Of course, she knew she would eventually be found, but the stares of normal people made her chest burn. All she wanted was a place away from the sunlight, but that was all the asylum provided. Its myriad of uncovered windows exposed her flesh to the shame of the sun.

None of the other patients paid her any mind. They twisted themselves through the corridors, women lost in their own spirals. Mary wondered if this truly was madness: isolation and fear left to fester too long.

Mary tracked a trail of slime down a new stairwell and through a heavy metal door. It led beneath the earth to a dark brick tunnel. Long pipes stretched like sinews down the hall and into the unknown. The pipes hissed, full of hot steam that misted the narrow space. Mary thought she would choke in it, but the only alternative was to return to the sun and the glare, so she shut the door behind her and continued.

She ventured deep, remembering the shame of her examination, the feeling of Dr. Edwards's observation, the scratch of his pen as he wrote on her chart. She scraped her nails at the brick walls, lit by single bulbs appearing sporadically down the corridor. Her bare feet slipped into the puddles, into the mud.

Past a fork in the tunnel, she heard humming. A song.

Mary, Mary, quite contrary...

She willed herself to go on, clawing her way further, turning corners, turning to glance back.

"Mary! Oh, Mary! How does your garden grow?"

She found the woman with the doll crouched beside a locked gate. The woman looked up at her, her smile of missing teeth like burrowing holes. She held the doll up to Mary and made it wave at her. "Would you like to see Mary's garden?"

The woman turned and pointed at a box full of dirt on the ground. Mary had to squint to see through the steam, but what lingered in the dirt was a cluster of red mushrooms. The woman plucked one from the soil and brought it to her lips. Then she picked another, and she held it out in offering. "If they knew about Mary's garden, they would take it away."

Mary shook her head.

"They call you Mary," she said, "but you can't be Mary. *She* is called Mary." The woman shook the doll and hummed.

Mary twisted her fingers into her gown, prying at the neckline, trying not to scratch. "Dr. Edwards calls me Jezebel," she said, her voice low.

The woman smiled. "Jezebel is a pretty name. A poisonous name." She offered the mushroom again.

This time, Mary took it, keeping the spore cradled in the warmth of her palm as she carried it back upstairs.

She found herself back in the recreation hall, where nurses and orderlies grabbed at her limbs and returned her to where she was supposed to be.

In her bed. In her room.

Her sterilized home.

She clutched the mushroom, protecting it from the light as the orderlies tethered her limbs. Her body told her to struggle, but she remembered the woman in the tunnel, who had already informed her that Mary no longer existed.

Mary was already dead.

She stared at the window at the glare of the sun, which shone over the asylum and the trees and the single road that led back into the village and, eventually, back to her cottage, where she had hidden for too long.

Further down the horizon, a mass of grey clouds gathered.

"Please," she begged, her voice echoing in the empty room. "Please help me."

At night, the door opened, and a white figure entered. Rubber soles squeaked over the tiles.

Mary turned in the black, squinting at the prints that Nathaniel left. He held a batch of gathered flowers.

He tossed them over her bed as though it was a grave.

Rain pattered against the window, and she drew a breath of moist air.

Nathaniel released her from her tethers, then pried the sheets off her body and pressed his lips against her ear. "Do you know why you belong here?"

Jezebel.

"You were isolated. Hysterical. Childless and alone and without purpose." His words hardened, raining spittle on her cheek. "I took pity on you, and you mistook that pity for lust."

"I mistook it for kindness," she said, her voice shaking.

"Only a whore would mistake the kindness of a well-established doctor, Mary."

She shook her head. "I had no idea you were a doctor."

"You are telling me that you willingly laid with a stranger," he said, lips curving into a smirk. "So, there must be some truth then, in what the nurses say? Have you bedded one of the orderlies yet?"

All of her wanted to shrink beneath his accusation, but instead she lifted a palm to his chest to see if he had a beating heart at all.

"You see?" he said, stepping out of reach. "There *is* quite the whore in this house."

A bead of water dripped from the ceiling and touched her forehead. She winced and forced herself to stand, lifting her gaze to the leak above. Nathaniel snatched her face in his hands, pinching her cheeks in his grasp. He mashed his fingers against her skull as though trying to reach inside.

"I had to fix you, Mary," he seethed. "I am going to fix you."

Her chest burned, and she imagined his strong hands carrying the dead tree away. She tried to fight, to push him back, but he shoved her atop the mattress and held her there until her limbs tired, her will dead, a place where mushrooms could fester. He watched her chest rise and fall and ground his jaw in frustration, in disgust.

"Jezebel," he spat.

He turned and left her untethered.

Rain poured in through the leak in the ceiling. It bled into the dirt he left behind, forming a puddle that grew through the night.

In the morning, Mary crawled from her bed, hands and knees over the muddy floor. She opened the bottom drawer of her dresser and gathered handfuls of dirt to pile over the crushed mushroom the woman had given her. Footsteps approached and she pushed the drawer closed just in time.

The nurse stared at the moisture on the floor, then glanced up at the leak that had spread across the ceiling overnight.

"Mary, what have you done?"

Mary kept her lips tight.

"Answer me, Mary."

It didn't matter how she answered. She'd never be able to turn the nurse's glare. It only hardened over her, and the nurse grabbed her elbow, dragging her from the room and into the narrow shower hall. She pried off Mary's gown and forced her beneath the spray of tepid water with a rough-bristled brush and a bar of soap.

"Clean yourself, Mary."

Goosebumps flocked Mary's skin like spores. She shrank beneath the water and stammered a plea of remorse.

"Clean yourself, or I'll have to do it for you."

So, Mary took the brush and ran the metal bristles down her arm.

"Not good enough," the nurse said, walking into the shower and yanking the brush from Mary's hand, forcing her onto the tiled floor so she could drag the bristles down her back. The soap stung against her flesh, made it boil and froth.

"Please! Please!"

But the nurse didn't stop until the burn spread all over, until the rashes had spread from her chest to her back. Once dry, Mary was given a crisp new robe, the starched fabric only irritating her fresh wounds.

"Let me get the doctor," the nurse said, taking Mary back to her room.

"No, please!" Mary pleaded, but the nurse returned with Nathaniel.

"My God, Mary," he said. "Look what's become of you." He withdrew another bottle of salve from his pocket, just like the bottle he'd given her before.

This time Mary wasn't given the chance to protest. The nurse held her down while Nathaniel applied the salve to her fresh wounds, the chemicals stinging, drawing cries of protest that sounded like leaves shaking in the trees.

He kept her confined to her bed so her skin could heal.

Hours passed with nothing to do but stare out the open door. Orderlies passed and leered, leaving their glistening trails behind. Some even tried to enter her room with a smile and a laugh and the muttering of her new name, but not before one of the nurses shooed them away.

"She is poisonous," they whispered. "Look at how red her skin is."

Day slipped into night, and with the night came more clouds and rain.

The black filled the ceiling again, dripping and forming new puddles on the marble floor.

Nathaniel came again. "You're not improving in the least," he said, pressing a thick layer of salve to her skin. "The nurses tell me things, Mary. They tell me what you do, that you leer at the men who pass, just as you did to me."

Mary shook her head.

"I know it resides inside of you," he said. "I saw it. Surely you must feel it in there, corrupting you."

He scratched at her stomach, his fingers curling, drawing blood.

She twisted against her binds, her flesh screaming. "Please!" she cried. "Please!"

"This is how you writhed beneath me," he said, pinching her, pulling at her skin like tree bark. "That is just how you begged."

Jezebel!

The rain pummeled the window, a rush of cold she forced herself to focus on until he released her and left the room, locking the door, leaving footprints in the dirt.

By morning, the moisture had seeped into her sheets and

pillow. It swelled the joints of the dresser, which allowed the mushroom spores to fester in the warmth of morning. Little red and white blotches peeked through the dirt and grew.

———

The nurse turned her nose at the state of Mary's room.

She stepped carefully over the earth and set a tray of food on her lap.

No porridge this time, but half of a fresh grapefruit, a boiled egg, and a slice of toast. A square of butter slid across the bread. But the orderlies came and took her by the arms, lifted her out of her seat and onto a gurney.

They wheeled her into a pastel yellow room filled with cabinets and machines and a bright light that glared in her face.

Nathaniel was already there.

Dr. Edwards was there, face brimming with determination as he lifted a new needle full of fluid.

"Please," Mary begged.

But he slid the needle into her arm, drawing his lips near and his breath to a whisper. "Jezebel, Jezebel, here on my pedestal, how does your perversion grow?"

The light glared, and Mary closed her eyes as she slipped away, imagining a lightning strike burning her isolated white cottage to ash.

———

A yellow room.

A glaring light.

Rain pattered against the skylight, and Mary turned her foggy head toward the medical table full of bloodied instruments. Among the clamps and tweezers and knives was a tray that held the piece of her that Dr. Edwards had removed.

Her heart thudded, but the red organ glistened in the tray like a full grapefruit scraped clean from its rind.

She struggled, but her arms were still strapped and splayed. She twisted her head and tried to sit up, though she was only able to lift her chin, peeking at the stitches keeping her midsection from splitting.

Dr. Edwards walked to the table with a smile, placing his gloved hand to her face, forcing her to look at the organ he'd removed. She squeezed her eyes shut, but his voice vibrated against her ear. "It was just as I thought, Mary. An infected demon with wings."

She tried to shake her head, but he pressed her cheek to the table.

"What do you say, Mary?"

Her vision blurred with tears. She struggled against her bindings, but the drugs made her spin, made her sick and dizzy. Her sobs echoed in the hollow room.

"Say it, Mary."

From the depths of her aching lungs, she found the words. "Thank you, Doctor."

A slug crawled along her window, leaving a glistening trail of slime.

The rain leaked through the growing hole in the roof. No one had cleaned her room, and its soaked, desolate state made Mary shiver. The base of the wooden dresser had started to rot, and the mushrooms chewed at the wood, growing fat and red and bulbous.

The nurse helped Mary sit, lip turned in disgust.

"He wants me to die," Mary said.

"Of course not," the nurse said, bringing Mary a tray of breakfast, which included the same breakfast she'd missed the day before. A slice of toast. A boiled egg with a saucer of salt. Another half of a fresh grapefruit. "Dr. Edwards has high hopes for your recovery. Now eat before your food spoils."

Mary ate, slipping her hand to the wound the stitches tried to contain. She imagined the emptiness inside as she slipped each segment of grapefruit past her tongue. The sinews burst and filled her mouth, but she tasted nothing. She applied the salt to her egg and bit into its overcooked hardness. The food piled inside of her belly, agitating her body, and she twisted in the bed and regurgitated compost onto the tiled floor.

Beside her, the nurse recoiled in disgust.

Another storm fueled the night. She got up and wandered the isolated space of her room, pressing her hands to the walls, spreading dirt across the sanitized surfaces.

Mary, Mary, quite contrary.

She blinked and hobbled, one hand still on her tender abdomen as footsteps started behind her.

She needed to leave.

She was not thriving.

She was not getting better, as Dr. Edwards had hoped. The footsteps came closer, and she found herself slipping through doors, the asylum a maze of dead-ends and tormenting spirals. She entered the stairs she'd tried to descend the first day she arrived. Rain clawed at the glass windows, glistening under the low light leaking in from the hall.

"Mary!"

His voice.

He yelled in the night, an accusation now, his growl like thunder in the hallway, his heavy steps beating in her chest. She got to the bottom and crept from the nearest door and into the courtyard.

The rain touched her skin. It chilled the heat inside her as she darted into the night, heading for the trees and the narrow gate.

She stared at the road that led back into town. She could run, could escape. She sped up her pace but felt the stitches pulling, thin threads tugging at her stressed skin. Blood seeped down the front of her gown. Her legs wobbled. She doubled over, her bare feet numbing in the mud.

The rain turned her hair to tendrils, dragging them down her shoulders. The leaves screamed in her ears, but she could still hear her name.

"Mary!"

Everyone knew where her cottage was. They would all come, would all call. They all knew who she was. What she was.

She turned to see his white coat waiting.

She walked toward his voice, her body just as foul as the woods that surrounded her.

———

They both left footprints walking back into the marbled halls of the asylum.

Lights flickered. Doors opened. People stared.

Mary, Mary, quite contrary. How does your garden grow?

Dr. Edwards left her in the care of the nurse, who ducked her beneath the shower again.

"You filthy whore," she said, scrubbing the brush over her skin, making it burn and boil to a poison shade of red.

The storm continued, even after she was led back to her room. Mary buried herself beneath the covers, curled her feet into the dirt in the sheets and sprouted roots.

———

The nurse brought a breakfast tray in the morning. On it was another boiled egg and a saucer of salt. No grapefruit, as she had nothing ripe within.

Mary didn't eat the egg, but she kept the salt clutched in her fist. The crystals melted in the heat of her palms. She licked at her fingers, which left her tongue raw and numb and craving sustenance.

She waited, hungry for Dr. Edwards to visit.

His coat was crisp, freshly bleached and starched with the appearance of cleanliness, yet his shoes sank deep into the mud of her room.

"You're truly beyond help, dear Mary." He left a glistening trail just like the slugs in her garden, coming for her overturned rind. He wrestled the chair from the vines in the corner and brought it before her bed. "Are you there, Mary?"

Sunlight cut through the window, warming the earth.

It was still her instinct to want to clean, but she grinned beneath his attention, slipped her bare foot through the mud and reached toward him. She curled her toes over the black leather of his shoe.

Dr. Edwards sat up straight. "Control yourself, Mary."

She leaned down and gathered a handful of earth. She pressed it between her fingers, ground the soil beneath her nails. She flattened her palm over his white coat, smearing grime over his heart. She pressed hard, gripped at his lapels, climbed over his lap.

His Adam's Apple bobbed in the angriest part of her.

"Mary," he tried.

"Jezebel," she said, slipping her poison fingers past his lips. She pried his mouth open and curled her reach inward, his screams turning shriveled as the salt burned him inside. "My name is Jezebel."

CHAPTER 10

LITTLE BLACK DEATH
1875

ORIGINALLY PUBLISHED IN *THE CROW'S QUILL* - ISSUE 01

The newest expansion of the Hargrove Mill opened the night Daniela was born. Gray smoke bloomed and blended into the sky as I labored. Daniela had my red hair, which I buried beneath the blanket when William entered my chambers to see his firstborn.

He took her and gazed at her sleeping face. He touched her cheek before facing the village below.

"I'm sorry," I said.

At this, he revealed the cold depths of his black stare to Daniela. It had seized me the day he brought his carriage to the village and proposed that I become his wife. His irises were as dark as his pupils, glistening with only the slightest touch of desperation as he waited for my response. My body had chilled, so fearful to answer. His lumber had built every structure in the village. He lived alone in his stone home, perched on the mountainside, each arched window accented with red draperies. When he kissed me on our wedding day, his mouth tasted of blood.

"What are you sorry for?" he asked, raising his gaze to my face full of tears.

"I-I know you only married me for an heir."

He placed Daniela back in my arms. His knee shifted the mattress as he leaned close and wiped the hot tears from my eyes. "Don't cry, darling. I married for love as well, and you've given me a daughter to spoil."

More tears came, clouding my eyes and turning the room into a swirl of red as he embraced us both. I tried to find comfort but felt only his chill. I smelled salt and iron, and the baby must have too, because she opened her mouth and screamed like a warning siren.

Villagers wrote open letters, telling William of their woes—their broken bones and broken families. The newspapers wrote of the ghastly conditions at the mill. Yet, after Daniela's birth, the newspapers wrote only of me. Columns described the expanse of the nursery, the wet nurses, and the myriad of servants at my disposal.

I made the mistake of reading the letters from other mothers. They complained of their hardships and their toil and their lost husbands. Their stories made me glance out the window at the factory. Weary workers filtered into the village, only to be replaced by another set of faceless men, like pieces in a machine of intricate cogs.

A siren rang, beginning the night shift. The smokestacks clouded the sky with gray haze. One of the maids came to shut the window. "That air's doing you no good, my lady."

"I used to breathe that air."

"You forget about that air once you've breathed this air." She scoffed at the village sitting in the valley, brewing, simmering, angry.

I had once been angry. I had once written letters of my own father's untimely death. But now my red hair blended with everything inside my husband's home, its fury lost behind the opulent curtains the maid pulled closed.

I demanded Daniela be christened at the village chapel. People watched us descend from William's carriage, my first time being seen not as a commoner, but as his wife. I glanced at the people I had once known, their faces now tenebrous and blurred. They gawked at my finery, at the bold brocade of my dress and the gold of my jewels. Mutters slipped through the crowds. *Traitor. Harlot.* The baby started to whimper.

One of the men stepped forward. "You come to gloat about your child, Mr. Hargrove, but what of mine?"

Others shouted from the crowd.

"The conditions at the factory are vile, Mr. Hargrove!"

My husband's stare hardened. His hand grew firm at my back.

"You use our church at your whim," another voice said. "You take one of our women and spoil her with the fruits of our labor! What do we ever get in return?"

William turned. "I pay you adequate wages. You all reside in modest homes. My wife even demanded I raise your wages and I did so, did I not?"

Voices rose. Fingers pointed. "We still pay with our own blood, sir!"

At this, the village roared.

Daniela cried in my arms, drawing the crowd's attention. William pulled my cloak over my head and pushed us through the carriage door.

The mob followed until the dirt roads of the village turned into the cobblestone path leading to our estate.

Servants locked the iron gate behind us, yet my fear didn't settle.

Daniela's screams drilled into my ears.

William handed her to the wet nurse. "They're ungrateful peasants," he snarled, his breath hot. "They might hate me, but they'll never hurt me or anyone I love." He clung to me like a possession, the fury we'd escaped only driving him to desire.

Later in his chambers, he tucked my hair behind my ear. "Are you grateful, darling?"

I did not answer.

Protests rose the night Victoria was born. Torchlight flickered in the streets as I labored. Victoria's red hair matched the crimson plumes rising between the tightly packed houses in the clouded village below.

This time, when William entered to see his second child, I did not apologize.

He took Victoria and moved to the open window, slamming the panes over the cries of those outside and pulling the red drapes over the darkness. The baby whimpered, but he rocked her gently and whispered in her ear. "Your mother thinks she has something in common with the workers. Perhaps, had she been more grateful for my love and devotion, you could have been a son."

"You could improve the factory conditions," I said firmly, remembering the fury with which I wrote my letters after my father's death.

William lifted his gaze, his expression hardening. "Their fires will always burn for me, darling, no matter what I do. I married you and I provided for you, and yet you still hate me as you did before."

Victoria cried, her fists tightening. William pressed a fingertip to her lips, and she bit down, jaw clenched tight. He nearly dropped her as he pulled free his bloodied finger. Victoria screamed, her lips parting to reveal teeth.

"My God," he gasped.

"You're a horrible, rapacious man," I said. "You're covered in blood. The entire house smells of it."

At this, he opened the chamber door and passed the baby to the waiting wet nurse. Then he came and wiped a rag against my sweat-soaked forehead. "You are red, my dear, but not with passion or desire or love, as you should be."

I turned, but he cupped my chin and forced me to drown in the black pit of his glare.

"I understand you care for the villagers, darling, but you don't live there anymore. You made a choice. All you have now is me."

He held me until his fingers trembled. Blood dripped down his hand from Victoria's bite, trickling against my neck. He tried to kiss me, but I denied him my love.

The newspapers wrote of the girls. Victoria bit like a snake. Daniela was shrill as a banshee. The articles described my fury, my temper. Columns detailed the fine silk and brocade of my gowns and the hours of labor that went into constructing them.

William had the papers brought to us at dinner. He read every article aloud. "She is said to be of fiery temper, snapping at even the slightest of inconsistencies. She is vapid. She is vile. She is vain."

He sipped our finest wine and continued until my face heated, and my tears flowed hot. Then he set his glass down and rose from the table. He shook my shoulders in his cold grasp and smiled. "You, my dear, are just as rapacious as I."

Riots started the night Adelaide was born. Hollers of tired men and mourning women sounded through the valley while I labored. Like her sisters, Adelaide bore red hair, which matched the bonfires burning in the village square. They built pyres and burned effigies in William's likeness, in my likeness, as well as little ones of the children.

A little girl with a gaping maw.

A toddler with sharpened teeth.

A baby, drenched in blood.

William entered the room and took Adelaide. She flailed, her brittle nails catching against his silk waistcoat. This time, he took her straight to the waiting nurse. He slammed the door and locked it. I made fists as the sirens rang, announcing another shift change at the mill. The roars from the village built into a crescendo.

William glared at me, his gaze making me shiver. "I did

what you wanted," he said. "I promised I would invest in new machinery, yet they told me it was too little, too late."

I turned to the window, where the torches and pitchforks came snaking up the path.

"They'll never make it past the gate," he scoffed. "Even if they did, there's a tunnel in the wine cellar that leads down to the docks."

"What then?" I asked, my voice shaking.

"We'll have each other." He kissed me, but I sat silent.

Moments later, the wet nurse banged on the door in tears. Adelaide refused to latch and had clawed her chest deep enough to draw blood.

"She's just like her mother," William said, leaving me alone with another little fire that burned at my breast.

Servants lingered in every corner, which only perpetuated gossip. I nursed Adelaide by the window, her scratches drawing me to tears. I distracted myself, surveying the factory and the village. It was from where I came, and yet these people knew nothing of my toil. I'd come from their bearings. I'd suffered their loss. I'd lost my father. I leaned out the window and screamed, but there was nobody close enough to hear. My throat burned. My body ached. I put the baby in her cradle and hurried to William's bed.

He kissed my tears and at the scratched and scabbed surface that Adelaide made of my chest. He licked at my skin, at the salt, the rust. "You taste like me, darling," he said, his touch cauterizing my tender flesh.

One of the remaining maids closed the window while I read in bed, sickened by the early stages of another pregnancy.

"You should stop reading those, my lady. They'll be the death of you, just as they were once the death of him."

"What do you mean?"

The maid smoothed the covers and smiled. "You'd written a letter about your father's accident. Mr. Hargrove raised wages, just as you'd demanded, yet the people still hated him. He then asked you to marry him. He said he admired your hair. It caught his eye and sent his heart aflutter."

I hesitated.

"Surely, you must understand his pain," the maid said.

"No," I said. She tried to take the paper, but I clung to the sheets. "I hardly feel a thing these days."

The factory burned the night Oliver was born. Villagers strode up the path to our mansion, torches bright and pitchforks raised. They wrestled with the wrought iron gate while I labored.

Unlike his sisters, Oliver had his father's dark hair, as well as the black pool eyes that drowned the worst of my misery.

William entered. He hurried to my bedside and pried the baby from my arms, his breath caught with emotion.

Outside, the villagers charged the gate, finally breaking the metal.

The remaining servants brought the girls to us, flailing and screaming, their mouths wide and shrill, teeth gnashing, claws bared.

I turned, but William was gone.

Oliver's scream echoed through the halls, down the stairs, and into the depths of the wine cellar.

William slipped through the secret door and closed it behind him, leaving spilt red over the stone floor.

I pounded on the door, but he locked it from the other side. "William! William, please! You're all I have!"

He did not respond.

He did not love me.

He was long gone by the time the villagers arrived, their pitchforks hungry for blood.

CHAPTER 11
IN HIS HANDS
1692

ORIGINALLY PUBLISHED IN *THE CROW'S QUILL* – ISSUE 02 (WITCHES & CAULDRONS)

Usually when Giles found a woman alone in the woods, he tackled her and had his way. Forearm to throat, he'd loom over their defeated figures. Their eyes begged and pleaded, only to bulge when their dying gasps acknowledged he was not a good man. He kissed them after and arranged sticks around them.

Witch's victims, the town thought.

Dorcas was different. She hissed and scratched. She called him evil, called him vile. She ripped hair from his scalp, so he smashed her head against a rock. She sank, eyes closed, not acknowledging him at all.

A crow called from the tree above. It cocked its head, curious.

Giles carried Dorcas home in darkness.

She woke when he threw her in the cellar. She didn't beg or plead. She just curled herself into the fetal position, whimpering in anticipation of what he might do.

Giles fell asleep to the sound.

By morning, her name had slipped through the village. The people prayed in circles, hoping she'd be found safe.

On the third day, Giles heard scrambling in the cellar. He

climbed down the rickety wooden steps with his lantern, waking his hostage.

A black rat squeaked.

Dorcas glanced at the creature before meeting his gaze. She curled herself into the corner, her skirts twisting up her legs, revealing the blood she'd spilled at the moon's call.

Giles stepped back, trampling the rat beneath his boot. Its death shriek clawed at his insides.

"Please do not look upon my shame," Dorcas begged, tugging at the stained linen.

He hurried back up the steps and brought her a bowl of water, a cloth, and a tunic. He gave her the lantern and looked away, giving her time to cleanse the blood from her skin.

She called on him in the morning. Another rat squeaked.

Giles got up with a hammer to kill the pest, throwing open the cellar door only to find Dorcas knelt in submission. The loose tunic hung off her narrow shoulders, exposing her skin to the candlelight.

He crouched before her and reached for the slender curve of her neck.

"Are you going to kill me?" she asked.

He wanted to. Her neck fit so perfectly in his grasp. Giles tightened his hold until her pulse raced against his fingers, beating in time with his. "You are naught like the others," he said.

The candle flickered, making her lips look like a smile. Women never smiled for him, so he wiped her lips to see if her smile was real.

A bell rang outside, somber and chilling.

There was another witch to hang.

He pulled the black hood over his head and went to the gallows to drape his noose over the neck of the accused. The crowd gathered close around the tree and roared.

The witch begged. She pleaded. She looked Giles in the eye but, through the hood, he was a nobody. A stranger.

He turned her body off the ladder.

The crowd roared as she struggled against the rope's unforgiving hold.

Giles wished it were his hands receiving glory instead.

He walked home.

A crow called down from the branches, cocking its head in mockery.

Giles unlocked the door to find that Dorcas had freed herself from the cellar.

She had prepared him dinner instead of escaping. She poured beer into a cup and ushered him into his seat. "Does this please you?" she asked.

Warily, Giles picked up his fork. The meat was tender and spiced, the bread hot and buttered. He sipped the beer, allowing the warming touch of alcohol to soothe the ache in his chest.

"It would please me more if you ate with me," Giles said, nodding at the empty chair beside him.

Dorcas shook her head and smiled a real smile, one that made his heart race. "I cannot eat with the devil." She placed a hand on his shoulder.

Giles winced, but Dorcas's brown eyes absorbed him. He couldn't look away.

"You are the devil," she said. "I searched for the devil in the woods, and you found me."

The meat turned rancid beneath his nose. He glanced at his plate, at the maggots that now twitched between the sinews. He groaned and pushed the plate back, bile filling his throat.

"Do I please you?" she asked, reaching for the drawstring of her tunic. She unwound it, freeing a shoulder, freeing her chest. She had a mole on her neck. A witch's mark. A place for the Devil to suckle. A place he desired most of all. "Are you my devil, Giles?"

He hesitated at first, smelling metal. Then he licked his lips. He eased out of his chair and stumbled to his knees before her.

She lowered the tunic further, allowing him to kiss her stomach, her breasts.

He rose and pressed his lips to her neck. He licked at the darkened teat, which satiated the need in him, the itch. A flood of warmth slipped into his veins. Desire captured his lungs, and he clung to her breathlessly, suckling at the savory taste of glory on her flesh. "I will never let you go," he said.

She wrapped her arms around him, cradling him as she took his ache away.

In the morning, Giles sat in the meeting house as the crowd searched another woman for marks. They tore at her clothes, and she twisted and shrieked. The people in the stands watched with wide eyes, faces red with rage. They pointed. They accused her of killing Dorcas, but the woman professed her innocence. She begged. Pleaded.

They called her a Proud Whore. The Devil's Slave.

A witch.

Giles knew he would be hanging her soon. The crowd's deluded desire clawed at his chest, driving all the blood to his loins. He removed himself from the court and quickly sought refuge in the woods. He unfastened his trousers and pressed his forehead to the trunk of a tree, trying to work his bestial lust into release.

Above him, a crow called.

Giles glanced up, trying to catch his breath.

The crow glared from the branch, its beaded black eyes like dark windows.

"*I* am the Devil," Giles said. "She hath called *me* her Devil."

The crow cocked its head.

He tried to kiss her lips, but she turned away.

"The Devil dost not kiss," she said. "My Devil licks. My Devil feasts upon my flesh." She combed her fingers through his hair and took a seat on the edge of the mattress. She removed her tunic and guided him to kneel so he could kiss the tender flesh between her thighs. Her skin was ripe with freckles, moles, passages in which he could lose himself.

He pulled her legs around him like walls. He licked her folds until her gasps of pleasure flooded warmth into his mouth. He drank until his thirst was wracked with heaving sobs.

The next morning, he pulled his noose over the throat of the newly accused witch.

She begged and pleaded. She took all the attention from the crowd.

Giles pushed her off the ladder and everything ceased. The chants faded.

The witch spun in circles, her reddened face becoming a blur.

All his power meant nothing without glory.

The crowd faded, leaving him alone with the witch's body. Usually, he left them up to set an example. This time, Giles cut her down and threw her into his wheelbarrow. He took her to the mountainside and stared into her empty eyes.

They didn't acknowledge him, looking to the gray clouded sky, where the crow cawed.

Giles refused to turn. He tossed the witch down the hillside and ran home to the woman who had pledged her life to him, her body a full feast of distraction.

A bewitched boy thrashed on the meeting house floor.

Giles watched him, certain he was only acting in an attempt to accuse the woman on the stand.

"She speaks to the animals! The creatures! She lets them suckle upon her!"

Giles swallowed. He couldn't catch his breath. Again, he removed himself. He passed through the woods, thinking only of Dorcas, his servant, his kept woman.

Usually, when Giles returned, he opened the door to find her naked in bed, her arms spread wide in offering.

This time, the sheets were stained with blood from between her legs. A rat squeaked. Dorcas cradled its girth in her palm. She cooed and gently stroked the rat's fur as it eagerly suckled upon the mole on her throat.

"Whore!" Giles cried. He ran to the bed, grabbing the rat. Its body contorted. It scratched at his arms, but he slammed it to the floor and hammered his boot to the creature's squeals.

Dorcas shifted, smile widening, her laugh filling the room.

"You are a witch!" he screamed, grabbing her throat. He pushed until her eyes bulged.

"My Devil!" she laughed. "Oh, my Devil!" She touched his shoulders, smearing blood on his face and tunic. "Drink upon me! All of me! All of my shame! Taste it, Giles! Drink upon me, you foolish man!"

She pushed his head between her legs, forcing him to lap at the red.

He was thirsty, so thirsty, so desperate for release. He drank with abandon, feeling as though he would starve if he didn't lick every drop of her wine.

He rolled over in the morning, mouth tasting of coins. Red was still pasted to his lips.

Dorcas lay asleep beside him. Rats shrieked around the bed.

He grabbed her hair and pulled her off the mattress, across the floor, to the center of town. He threw her naked figure upon the ground and pointed. "She's a witch!" he cried. "She bewitched me! She seduced me!"

The people came, voices wary. Whispers fluttered, but Giles shouted the truth until the congregation dragged her to the jail.

She hollered and shrieked like the others. Her screams beat at the overcast skies.

He followed, his heart throbbing, his chest aching.

The only way to soothe the pain of his jealousy was to rage with the mob.

"The Devil's Slave! A Proud Whore!"

He forced himself to cry during his testimony.

"She found me in the woods. I could not help but take her home. She stole my appetite. She filled my home with vile creatures and made me feast upon her. She let the rats feast upon her. I beg for forgiveness!"

It was all the people needed to convict her.

Days later, he held Dorcas on the ladder, black hood over his head.

Only Dorcas knew he was Giles Downing, the town's killer. The Devil.

It was all he had wanted in the beginning. He tightened his grasp around her waist, thinking of the rat, the way it had sat so lovingly perched on her palm. His chest burned and he pushed her off the ladder, away from his hold and into the strangle of the noose.

Dorcas drew a breath instead of choking. "The Devil is in me!" she cried. "The Devil taketh me!" Her body contorted. Her muscles clenched and flexed. She writhed against the rope, which was no longer an extension of Giles's hand. Her breasts heaved. Her muscles spasmed. Her eyes begged, pleaded, only to bulge in delight when Death's caress finally combed her body with undulations of gracious release.

Giles felt no blood in his loins. He felt no need for glory, only the penetrating weight of shame against his chest. Desperately, he rushed to cut her down.

He laid her down on the dirt, her lips spread into a grin. Her pulse no longer beat with his. Her dead eyes stared not at him, but at the sky, where a crow watched from the tree.

It cawed and cocked its head, its black eyes glistening, reflecting him, a cuckold.

ACKNOWLEDGMENTS

Writing a book is always a mix of solitude and solitary confinement, so I'd like to thank those who supported me when I really needed it most over the last couple of years.

To my beloved former coworkers, especially Kim, Nancy, Deb, Lynn, Jenny, Julia, Frank, Anu, Rana, Dorothy, Nicole, and Ron, (among so many others!) for always showing interest in my writing career, and for always believing that I was doing something worthwhile.

To my church friends, Sarah, Justin, Corey, David, Krupa, and Pastor Shelley. What I write about might not be wholesome, but I appreciate all the moments you listened and supported me through all the highs and lows.

To my writer pals who I've known for years but never met in person. Thank you to Richard Thomas, Jessica McHugh, Jessica Taylor, Caitlin Moreau, Nathaniel Blackburn, and Sadie Hartmann. Your support and kind words give me such a serotonin boost, and make me so happy to have found a place within the horror community.

Much love to everyone at Quill & Crow Publishing House. Being a Canadian writer at times gives me such cabin fever. There's nobody up here to hang out with, but the best reward has been finding like-minded people to work with. Thank you to Eli for your helpful line edits. Thank you to October Comics and Fay for the glorious cover design. Thank you William and Rho for working with me on my contributions to *The Crow's Quill*. Thank you to Alma, Rosalyn, Mel, and Jax, for all your live chats and marketing expertise. A very big thank you to Cassandra for reading *Woman of the White Cottage* all the way through. None of this would have happened if you didn't.

Lastly, to my family, who bears the brunt of my absences.

Thanks to my husband, Jon, and my kids, Maggie and Arthur, for letting me sit at the dining room table with headphones in. Thanks to my parents for doing your best to understand why I made writing my career. Thanks to my sister, Rachael, and my cousin M.C, for the beta reads. Sharing my work with relatives has been difficult, and I very much appreciate family eyes on my work.

Salamat po.

ABOUT THE AUTHOR

Rebecca Jones-Howe is the Fil-
ipino-Canadian author of *Vile
Men*. Her short fiction has ap-
peared in, among others, PANK,
Dark Moon Digest, Peachfuzz
Magazine, *The New Black*, *Lost
Contact*, and *Human Monsters*.
She resides in Kamloops, British
Columbia with her husband and
two children.

Also by Rebecca Jones-Howe:
Vile Men

TRIGGER INDEX

The Red House - domestic abuse (mentioned), emotional abuse, suicide (mentioned), alcoholism, Covid isolation

Hostages - hostage situation, PTSD, physical violence (choking), alcoholism, gore, suicide

A Patient, A Guest - domestic abuse (mentioned), self-harm, eating disorder, suicide, sexual content

The Lantern - alcoholism, murder, sexual content, violent content (stabbing), suicide, gore

A Lesson in Sophistication - sexual abuse, self-harm, grooming

Honeymoon - graphic sexual content, domestic abuse

The Walking Hours - death (infant), PTSD

The Fruits of Wartime - sexual content, physical violence (choking)

Woman of the White Cottage - sexual content, forced hospitalization, forced medical procedures, surgery

Little Black Death – bullying, character assassination, death (mentioned), abandonment

In His Hands - witch prosecution, sexual content, kidnapping, rape (implied), murder (hanging)

THANK YOU FOR READING

Thank you for reading *Ending in Ashes*. We deeply appreciate our readers, and are grateful for everyone who takes the time to leave us a review. If you're interested, please visit our website to find review links. Your reviews help small presses and indie authors thrive, and we appreciate your support.

Other Titles by Quill & Crow

Anomalies & Curiosities

The Blood Bound Series

Haunted: A Crow Showcase

Printed in the USA
CPSIA information can be obtained
at www.ICGtesting.com
JSHW021607080923
47978JS00002B/14